Fernando realized he'd pushed too hard with Nicole.

He'd tried so hard to get her to understand his way of thinking—and forgive him. He should have been more gentle and patient with her, rather than demanding.

"How will this stop her from biting?" Nicole asked, looking up from Snookie.

He felt Nicole's horse tense as he felt along the ridge on her back. "Horses bite for a lot of reasons. She's exploring, but she also knows it's a good way to protect herself. We just have to show her that she doesn't need to protect herself anymore."

As Nicole nodded once again, he saw more confidence in her eyes. She seemed more open and less afraid. Like the lessons that were healing Snookie were working in Nicole's heart, as well.

Maybe he and Nicole would never get to a place where things were good between them. But he would do everything in his power to make sure her heart didn't get broken again…

Danica Favorite loves the adventure of living a creative life. She loves to explore the depths of human nature and follow people on the journey to happily-ever-after. Though the journey is often bumpy, those bumps refine imperfect characters as they live the life God created them for. Oops, that just spoiled the ending of Danica's stories. Then again, getting there is all the fun. Find her at danicafavorite.com.

Books by Danica Favorite

Love Inspired

Three Sisters Ranch

Her Cowboy Inheritance
The Cowboy's Faith

Love Inspired Historical

Rocky Mountain Dreams
The Lawman's Redemption
Shotgun Marriage
The Nanny's Little Matchmakers
For the Sake of the Children
An Unlikely Mother
Mistletoe Mommy
Honor-Bound Lawman

Visit the Author Profile page at Harlequin.com for more titles.

The Cowboy's Faith

Danica Favorite

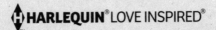

HARLEQUIN® LOVE INSPIRED®

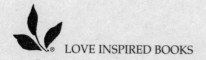

LOVE INSPIRED BOOKS

Recycling programs
for this product may
not exist in your area.

ISBN-13: 978-1-335-47929-7

The Cowboy's Faith

Copyright © 2019 by Danica Favorite

www.Harlequin.com

Printed in U.S.A.

Trust in the Lord with all thine heart;
and lean not unto thine own understanding.
In all thy ways acknowledge him,
and he shall direct thy paths.
—*Proverbs* 3:5–6

For George Funk, thanks for all of your friendship and support with our horses. I appreciate how you always answer our questions, both about our horses, and for my books. And thanks for always looking for my books to give to Julie. Our family is blessed to have your family in our lives.

And for all the inmates, trainers and staff at the Wild Horse Inmate Program in Cañon City as well as those at the Wyoming Honor Farm. We are so thankful for the incredible animals we have, thanks to the training our horses got from you. I pray your time with the horses has blessed you as it has blessed us.

Chapter One

The foolish woman was going to get herself killed.

Fernando Montoya parked his truck and jumped out, then ran to the arena where Nicole Bell was working a bay mare. Clearly green, the mare looked terrified. Like she had no idea what was happening to her. Based on Nicole's jerky movements, Fernando had to agree with the mare. Nicole seemed to be clueless as to what she was doing.

As he got closer, he slowed his pace, knowing that his panic would scare the horse even more. He forced himself to calm his breathing as he drew near.

"Hi, Nicole."

He spoke quietly, softly, but Nicole spun as if he'd shouted.

"What are you doing here?" she asked.

He'd just wanted to make sure Nicole was okay.

Columbine Springs was barely twenty minutes out of his way—a short stopover on his way from Denver to southern Colorado to a new job with his uncle's construction company. It would be another two hours to his destination, but it was worth it to take the detour. The tiny ranching town with its fertile grassland surrounded by mountains had little to recommend it, other than a faded-out sign for an ice-cream place that promised the best cones in the Rockies. No reason to stop, other than the fact that this run-down ranch just off the highway was where Nicole and her two sisters now lived.

He wouldn't stay long, just long enough to reassure himself that Nicole's excuses of being too busy with her new ranch to talk were true.

After all, he had a new life of his own to get to. At least that's what he kept telling himself. The job was menial work, something a trained monkey could do, but it was all that was available to him, thanks to the inexperience of his youth.

One felony conviction. That's all anyone saw on his employment applications, even though he'd done his time, was a hard worker and hadn't been in any trouble in the four years since he'd gotten out. No one wanted to know the circumstances of his crime or that he was truly sorry for his mistake.

He'd give anything to right the wrongs of his past, but he couldn't, so all he wanted to do now was find a way to build a future for himself, even if it wasn't the future he'd planned.

Not that he could share that with Nicole. His employment woes weren't something he shared with anyone, least of all the reasons for them.

"I was on my way to just south of Salida, where my uncle lives. Thought I'd stop by to see how you were doing. I heard you and your sisters inherited a ranch from a long-lost relative or something like that."

Though he'd once been told Nicole's eyes were hazel, they looked almost green with the anger flashing in them. She brushed her dark hair out of her face—it was falling out of its ponytail, and, judging from the sweat dampening the edges of her hairline, she'd been at this for a while. Though it was only May, the sun was hot, and the work hard.

"That's right," she said. "I've always wanted to get out of the city, have a few animals, live the good life."

The tension in her voice told him her current life was anything but good. And, in the few terse conversations they'd had over the past year or so, he'd been wondering how she was really doing. Nicole hadn't been the same since his sister, Adriana, and Nicole's fiancé, Brandon, had run off together, leaving Nicole at the altar and dying in a car accident in the process. Nicole might say everything was fine, but she was clearly struggling.

Even in this momentary interaction, despite her anger, he knew he'd been right to stop by. Only someone with a death wish would work such a green horse in this manner. Her absolute stupidity in how she was handling the horse made him think something deeper was going on, because Nicole wasn't stupid.

"I was worried about you," Fernando said. "And, it seems, rightly so. That horse is dangerous, and you'll get both of you hurt, if not killed."

She stared at him like he was as crazy as he thought she was. "I saw this on a horse training video. It's exactly what the trainer did."

Similar, but not exact. He knew the training she spoke of. Had watched the same video series. "You're holding the rope wrong. Angle the horse outside your space, rather than letting her push you around. Turn your body the other way."

She did as he asked, and immediately the horse started to respond. Not perfectly, because the mare had already been taught bad habits, but at least Nicole was in the right position to correct her.

The horse invaded Nicole's space and tried nipping at her, but Nicole stepped away in time.

"No," Fernando said. "She just completely disrespected you. You never want the horse to think she's in control. It's also a bad sign that her response to you is to bite. You've got to break that habit."

He entered the arena and took the rope. "Here. Let me show you."

Nicole gave him control of the horse, frustration in her eyes. He went through the same exercise Nicole had been trying, establishing rapport with the horse, but not by letting the mare walk all over him.

She was a spirited one, and someone like Nicole, who had never been around horses as far as he knew, was ill suited to take care of this horse, let alone train her.

"Why are you here?" The look of loathing she gave him almost made him want to turn and run.

But he'd seen the expression before. He deserved it. After all, he'd known about Adriana's involvement with Brandon. He'd warned Adriana against dating her best friend's fiancé and told her she was playing with fire. Adriana had told him to mind his own business, and that she knew what she was doing.

He'd seen Nicole nearly a dozen times since finding out about Adriana and Brandon, and yet, every time he opened his mouth to try to tell her what was going on behind her back, he found the words didn't come. He'd spent too many years fearing punishment for opening his mouth about other people's business.

Sometimes he woke up in the middle of the night, asking himself why he hadn't done more. He'd already shamed his family so much, first by going to prison, and now this. If he had only said something, maybe Adriana and Brandon would at least still be alive.

He couldn't change the past, but maybe he could do something about the future. The job his uncle wanted him on wasn't going to start for another month. But Fernando's apartment lease was up, so he'd figured he'd head to his uncle's early and get the lay of the land.

But he could use that time to do some good instead.

"Let me work with your horse," he said, ignoring her question. "I can do it. You've already seen the results."

Her sister Leah approached. "I agree. Shane thinks you've taken on too much with this horse. With the extra cattle we have this year, he doesn't have the kind of time he needs to put into training her."

Nicole gave an exasperated sound. "Ever since you and Shane got together, it's always Shane this, Shane that. I thought we all agreed we didn't need some man to rescue us. And I certainly don't need this one."

Her words sounded full of pain, and it made him feel worse, knowing that because of Brandon, and because of Fernando's role in the situation, she directed her anger at all men.

But this wasn't about him, or men, but about a horse who needed his help. "I was wrong in not telling you about Adriana and Brandon sooner, but surely you can put our personal differences aside and allow me to help you with this horse."

Nicole glared at him. "It's not just about that. I mean, it is. It seems like everybody thought they knew what was best for me but never once asked my opinion. Just like now. I've told you that I don't want you in my life. But here you are, insisting on helping me. Can't anyone respect the decisions I make for myself?"

He hadn't thought of it that way. But how could he explain his genuine concern? That even though she pretended she was fine, and told everyone she was, he could see the pain in her eyes, hear it in her voice.

"I'm truly sorry for disrespecting your wishes. But you saw how the horse responded to me. I appreciate your passion for animals and that you want to work with them, so let me teach you what I know. You've got a great foundation by watching the videos and reading the books, but nothing can replace the real-life experience of handling a horse with someone who's been trained to do so and learning from that expertise."

She hesitated, then took a step forward. "Do you really think you can help me? How can I be sure you know what you're doing? The horse's response could have just been coincidence."

Her voice faltered as she spoke, and he knew she wasn't so much telling him as herself. She wanted his help, but she also wasn't ready to admit it.

"At least give me the opportunity to try. I can talk with this Shane person and let him evaluate me." He looked over at Leah. "From what you say, he knows about horses."

Leah smiled at him. "Yes. Shane Jackson is my fiancé and owns the ranch next door. We rely on him for his ranching expertise. He was good friends with Helen, our ex-stepmother, who left my sisters and me the ranch when she died."

Nicole groaned, and Leah turned to glare at her. "What's your problem? Shane was just saying that unless you got Snookie's tantrums under control and she stopped biting, you'll have to get rid of her. It's not safe to have her here with the boys. He's the horse expert, so I fully trust his judgment where Snookie is concerned."

Fernando remembered Leah's two little boys, Dylan and Ryan, from Nicole's rehearsal dinner. Cute little fellows, and though saying so would rile up Nicole further, Leah was right. The mare's jerky movements made her too unpredictable to be around small children. He'd already seen her try to bite Nicole. A horse like that was dangerous.

"He doesn't need to be in on our personal business," Nicole muttered.

He knew way more personal things about Nicole than Nicole probably wanted him to know—or thought he knew. The matter of their living circumstances paled in comparison.

But he didn't think saying so would endear him to Nicole. The mare jerked at the rope, and had it been Nicole holding her, she'd have gotten away. Nicole's technique was too loose, and she seemed ill prepared to handle these outbursts. As it was, Fernando was going to have some killer rope burns on his hands.

He tied the horse up at the fence, then turned his attention back to Nicole.

"I don't need to be acquainted with your personal

business to know this horse needs help," Fernando said. "I know you've always wanted a horse and that letting this one go would break your heart. But I agree with Shane. It's not safe to have a horse like this around your nephews unless she gets some intensive training."

Leah murmured something under her breath and nodded.

He'd always thought Nicole's eldest sister was also smart, so maybe she would talk some sense into Nicole.

And maybe it was overstepping to think so, but he wasn't sure this beautiful, fragile woman who acted so tough could stand to have her heart broken again.

Nicole fought tears at his words. But she wasn't going to let Fernando—or anyone else—see her cry. Part of her wanted to scream at him and shake him for being such a thick-headed dolt. So he knew that giving up this horse would break her heart? And he wanted to help? Where was that help when her best friend was messing around with her fiancé?

Okay, fine. She got it. Fernando had called her time and again, begging for forgiveness and for the chance to make it up to her. So here it was. His chance to make things right.

But why did helping her horse have to be the means of fixing his guilt? What about her pain? Fernando got absolution, and she was still left alone, minus a best friend and the man she'd thought she was going to spend the rest of her life with.

People liked to say that she was better off, and she didn't disagree. But the problem with such deep betrayal was that now she no longer knew who to trust.

It wasn't like when you became friends with someone new, they would answer the question "Are you a man-stealing backstabber?" honestly.

The only people Nicole could trust were her two sisters, Erin and Leah, and, she supposed, since Leah had fallen in love with him despite her painful past, Shane.

Which left the animals. They didn't lie to you, steal your fiancé, sneak behind your back or keep the kind of secrets that would break your heart.

She walked over to Snookie and gave her a pat. How was she supposed to give up on this horse, a sweet mare who just needed someone to love her? True, she did have her tantrums and liked to bite. She'd broken out of her stall more times than Nicole could count. And she'd even bitten one of the boys. That was the reason Shane had told her to get rid of Snookie.

But Nicole couldn't bear it. Something inside her said that she and Snookie belonged together, and even though everyone told her she was crazy, she could feel Snookie speaking to her the day she got her.

She needed Snookie, and Snookie needed her.

Fernando came over and took her hand, placing it on Snookie's flank. "Give her a firm rubbing here. It will help her feel more secure. She senses your emotions, and she needs to perceive that you're not upset with her."

The simple change of motion brought a shift to Snookie's posture, relaxing her.

"I'm sorry for upsetting you," Fernando said. "I know you don't believe me, but I've only ever wished the best for you."

Nicole stared at her feet. "I wish I could believe that, but I don't know how to believe anyone anymore."

"I understand," he said softly. "Maybe it's too much to ask you to have a little faith, but would you at least give me the chance to prove it to you? I can help your horse."

He already had, getting Snookie to respond better in just a few short interactions than she had with weeks of training. But why did it have to be him?

Just this morning she'd been praying, asking God to help her find a way to keep Snookie. She'd even gone so far as to call some of the local boarding facilities, to see if they had space for her. But word had already gotten out about her misbehaving horse, and no one wanted to take a chance on having her there, disrupting their space.

Was God's answer to her prayer really the person she despised the most in this world?

Fernando had gone around to the other side of Snookie and was touching her in swift, firm motions, like what she'd seen on some of the horse training videos.

"I've already done that with her," Nicole said.

Fernando continued the motions, not looking at her as he said, "Not enough. You can't rush or skip any of the steps in training a horse. It's easy to think a horse is ready, but you must exercise patience to look for signs that will tell you when they really are."

She'd heard one of the trainers on one of the videos say something similar, but he'd only spent fifteen minutes on this part of the training.

As Fernando continued with the exercise, his hands brushed her again, and she jumped back at the unexpected jolt.

"I'll just get out of your way," she said.

Fernando's dark brown eyes were all too human in the emotions she thought she spied. She walked slowly backward to the fence, not liking the idea that Fernando was anyone other than the person she'd been vilifying over the past year.

But she couldn't help looking. Seeing the dark hair with waves that would probably be similar to the gentle curls Adriana used to hate for being too unruly to do much with put a pang in her heart over the loss of her friend. It was hard not to notice how much Fernando resembled Adriana.

It was even harder noticing how he didn't. Like the softness and gentleness in his face, and the tenderness with which he spoke to Snookie. And to Nicole.

Adriana used to say that he was the best big brother in the whole wide world and that she didn't know how she could ever live without him. Watching Fernando now, Nicole couldn't help remembering all the reasons she'd loved Adriana, and it made her heart hurt to allow that crack in the walls she'd kept around herself to numb the pain.

Because that's what no one understood. Nicole had gone from one day believing that she was marrying an amazing man, and that she couldn't imagine having a better best friend than Adriana, to realizing that they'd both betrayed her in the worst possible way. She'd lost so much and had no idea why.

"He's amazing, isn't he?" Leah said, nudging Nicole. "He's like that guy Shane took us to see, only better."

"I'm sure we can't afford him. We couldn't afford the other guy," Nicole said.

"Maybe he'll give us a friend discount." Leah's voice sounded hopeful, and it hurt to realize that her sister didn't understand the problem.

"We're not friends," Nicole said.

Leah sighed. "It's not good for you to keep holding a grudge. I get it. What his sister did was terrible, and yes, it was awful of him to not tell you. But anyone can see how bad he feels, and maybe, rather than taking your grief out on him, the two of you could grieve together?"

Nicole spun to face her sister. "What are you saying?"

"Did you ever think that he's lost someone, too? That he's also hurting? You keep making this all about you, but maybe if you let someone else in, you'd realize that you're not alone."

The tenderness in Leah's eyes made it impossible for Nicole to be angry with her. But it didn't mean Leah was right. Yes, Leah knew what it was like to suffer tragedy, and she knew what it was like to lose someone she loved. But Nicole's pain was different, and to suggest that Fernando would share it was absolutely ridiculous.

Leah reached out and touched Nicole's shoulder gently. "I'm sorry if I'm pushing too hard, but even if you can't accept that Fernando might need you just as much as you need him, you can't deny that he's doing wonders with your horse."

Nicole turned around to watch Fernando work with the horse, and as she leaned against the rails, from the other side of the fence, Leah put her arm around Nicole.

Leah didn't have to say anything, and even though Nicole was still technically mad at her sister, she knew Leah loved her. And as she relaxed into her sister's embrace, Nicole realized that she couldn't fight the situation anymore.

Nicole loved Snookie and desperately wanted to keep her horse. But she knew Shane was right. Snookie was a danger to her nephews. Fernando's interaction with Snookie told her that he was probably her last hope in being able to keep the horse.

If God wanted to answer her prayers with the person who reminded her most of her heartbreak, then fine. Let Him. She'd accept Fernando's help with Snookie, but there was no way she'd give him access to her heart.

Chapter Two

The mare pawed at the ground and tugged at the rope. Fernando had been holding her back, and she was getting impatient at being restricted. She reminded him of the horses he'd trained in prison. Straight off federal lands, the wild mustangs had to learn how to be part of the human world.

"She doesn't like you," Nicole said, sounding petulant as she stepped forward. "Let me take her back."

No, *Nicole* didn't like him. Her attitude toward him was less about the horse and more about her personal feelings toward him. The horse was still figuring him out, deciding whether or not she could trust him. He would earn this horse's trust, and maybe Nicole's.

"She's angry that she cannot be free to do what she wants. But like a child, she must learn that we have rules to keep her safe. Once she learns that we mean her no harm, she can develop a respect for humans, and she'll be easier to work with."

Maybe Nicole and the horse weren't so different.

He brought the horse in to him and began touching her. "Hey, Snookie girl. We're going to help you learn, okay?"

Not all trainers talked to the horses, but for a long time, horses had been the only creatures Fernando could trust. Conversations with them were easier than with people.

Probably why Nicole was channeling all her grief into the run-down ranch. Though Fernando could see places on the house that had obviously been recently repaired, new fences mixed in with the old, there were also a lot of broken-down outbuildings, worn-out equipment and other signs of neglect. He knew they had inherited the ranch from a long-lost relative, but until Leah had mentioned it, he hadn't known it was a former stepmother.

Judging from the condition of the ranch, the woman had probably been too old to take proper care of things. Though he knew that Leah and their other sister, Erin, had also gone through tragedies around the time of Nicole's failed wedding, and it probably seemed like a good idea to all of them to escape Denver and come here for healing, he had to wonder if they'd all taken on more than they could handle.

Maybe he could help them fix things up while he was here. He had nothing better to do until the job with his uncle started in a month, and even then, he wasn't excited about it. Unskilled labor, acting as a helper to the better-paid framers on his uncle's crew. Though Fernando had years of construction experience, he'd been let go from his last job as a foreman with a large construction firm in Denver because he couldn't pass the background check they needed to get clearance on one of their jobs. And he hadn't been able to get hired elsewhere because of his record.

Though he was grateful his uncle was offering him a job, he was also a bit resentful that Sergio knew of his skill but was taking advantage of his desperation and offering him something so beneath him. Fernando would probably end up doing the job of the foreman while accepting the pay of a helper. His uncle was a known cheapskate, and he recognized Fernando had no other options.

It was too bad Fernando couldn't get a job working with horses. Fresh out of prison, he'd tried, thinking that the horse training he'd done there would give him the necessary qualifications. And it did—to an extent. But just like with construction work, people saw the felony on his record and used it as either an excuse to pay him peanuts or not hire him. Or worse, if something went wrong, the felon was always the convenient scapegoat. So he'd gone back into construction, something he'd done since he was young, hoping that someday he'd have enough money to buy a small place and a couple of horses for himself.

The familiar motion of working the horse blocked out all the nagging thoughts. He touched Snookie's back firmly, assuring her that he was there and he wasn't going to hurt her. The harsh breath coming out of the horse's nostrils slowed, and he could feel the rhythm of her heartbeat.

As he ran his hand along the horse, looking for sensitive places, she tensed up under his touch. A couple of unusual places for most horses, but to Fernando, they told a story. A sad story of someone who had asked too much, too soon, and hurt her when he didn't get it.

"Who hurt you, girl?" he asked softly, touching her in another way to comfort her. He said a prayer that God would guide him and lead him as he helped her. *Lord, show me exactly what I need to do to help this horse.*

As he began the process of earning her trust, he could feel her leaning in and trusting him more. He continued bringing her through the exercises. She was a smart horse, a good horse, and she already knew all the things he was trying to teach her.

Snookie calmed down, and once she had settled, he knew it was time to stop.

He turned to Nicole. "We should put her away for the day. She's been worked hard, but we're in a good place."

She stared at him. "What just happened there? I've seen things like that on videos, but never in person."

"That was amazing," Leah said, coming around Nicole. "I've never seen that horse so calm."

He gave a quick nod to acknowledge Leah's compliment, even though he'd done nothing special. Anyone trained to work with mustangs could have done what he just did, but it seemed rude to say so.

Nicole frowned. "How do you even have experience with horses? Adriana said the only horses you were interested in were under a car's hood."

He figured he'd get this question, but he wasn't ready to answer it.

"There are a lot of things you don't know about me, just as I'm sure there are things I don't know about you. I've spent a great deal of time working with horses, and

I've been trained by some of the best. Maybe if we took some time to learn about each other…"

Nicole's face darkened. "I don't want to get to know you. I thought I made it very clear that I don't want you in my life. You're just here to help Snookie."

His only concern was with making sure she was safe. But it was hard not to take her attitude toward him as a challenge. A defiant horse was often a hurting horse. Which made him wonder if her treatment of him was about her deeper pain. Could he help Nicole as well as the horse?

Even though she'd just told him she only wanted his help with Snookie, he couldn't help but smile in response to her words.

Of all the nerve.

She'd just told him she didn't want him here, and he'd smiled. Smiled!

"Let's get Snookie put away," he said. "And we can worry about the rest later."

She'd have liked to have come back with a snappy retort or something, but Nicole could tell that her irritation was grating on her sister's nerves. Leah had questioned her negativity earlier, and it wasn't really directed at her sister, but she'd taken it that way.

Mostly, Nicole's life was good. Other than the fact that she was still struggling with her fiancé and best friend running off together and getting themselves killed. Oh yeah, and they'd been carrying on behind her back for months.

Fernando could've saved her a whole lot of humiliation and heartbreak, and maybe even kept Brandon and Adriana from dying because they wouldn't have needed to run off together in the middle of the night. They could've just been together in the open, because Nicole would've dumped Brandon's sorry self and told Adriana thanks but no thanks.

But apparently, Fernando wasn't willing to give her credit for being strong enough to deal with that information. Clearly, he didn't think she could handle her horse, either. But he'd already proven that he knew way more about horse training than she did, so she couldn't tell him to bug off.

"Her stall's this way," Nicole said, taking the rope out of his hands and leading the horse. He might have shown some skill in training, but this was her horse.

Fernando nodded and stepped in line behind her.

Why did he have to be so agreeable? It was like he knew she was only grudgingly allowing him to be here, and he was doing his best to make her like him.

She took a deep breath and willed the threatening tears to stay back. She wouldn't cry over this. Especially not in front of anyone else. Nicole's job in the family had always been to make them smile. Maybe it wasn't her official title, but that's what she knew her sisters counted on her for. Being cheerful, happy and the life of the party.

Maybe that was who she used to be, but it wasn't who she was anymore. The animals were the only safe things in her life. More important, they weren't telling her what to do, how she should live her life. They just let her be her, without judging her.

Fernando opened the barn door for her, a task she

could have done on her own, but he seemed determined to prove that he could help her.

So Fernando felt bad about what happened? Good for him. Maybe he thought that by doing a few good deeds for Nicole, everything would be all right. But it didn't work that way. And even though everything that happened technically wasn't his fault, it was nice to have someone to blame, since the real people she was mad at were dead.

She led Snookie into her stall and removed the halter. "There you go, girl. Nice job today. Are you ready for your supper?"

It was tempting to add that the silly horse was a traitor, falling so easily for her sworn enemy's charms. Because he was charming. And once, back when her life seemed simpler, she'd even joked to Adriana that were Nicole not happily engaged, she'd have thought Fernando a hottie.

"I can help, if you like. Two flakes of hay?"

Once again, Fernando was trying to be helpful. Were it any other person, she wouldn't feel so much resentment about his assistance. In fact, she'd be grateful.

But this was the man who symbolized all her pain.

And yes, she knew all the classic psychological speak for everything going on. People acted like she was stupid because she was a preschool teacher. But she did have her master's, and she'd taken enough psychology courses in the process to grasp all the technical details about what she was dealing with. All the classic stages of grief.

"Yes," she muttered, trying not to sound like such an ingrate. Were a stranger to peek into her life, they might think she was a horrible person for how she was treating Fernando.

In a way, she kind of felt that way about herself. But the pain in her heart was like a throbbing headache that only got worse when Fernando was near. Right now, it was like the kind of migraine that made you throw up.

Once Snookie was fed, Leah invited Fernando into the house for a glass of iced tea while they waited for Shane to come over, making the pain in Nicole's heart even worse. Throwing up was almost an option. But instead, Nicole smiled. And she meekly followed them into the house, keeping the smile firmly planted on her face while figuring out how she was going to handle accepting help from the person she despised the most.

No, it probably wasn't the most healthy thing for her to be doing, but it felt a whole lot better than falling apart over something that could never be fixed.

Fortunately, Shane didn't take too long in arriving.

"Sorry I couldn't get here sooner. The fence on the back pasture is down in a few spots, and I wanted to get it fixed before you guys moved the herd there tomorrow."

Shane's engagement gift to Leah had been a herd of cattle that had initially come between them but was now what the sisters had hoped would be the start of turning their property back into a real working ranch. Which seemed like an impossible dream, considering they only had one horse, and that horse was not yet able to work the ranch. But on their budget, finding what Shane called a good horse seemed next to impossible.

Leah gave Shane a quick hug and kiss. "Oh, good.

Erin took the boys over to the Double R Ranch to borrow a couple of ATVs so we can get the herd moved."

Then Leah gestured at Fernando. "I want you to meet Fernando Montoya, an old family friend who says he can help with Snookie."

Nicole would have liked to have argued with Leah about the *old family friend* part, but since Shane and Fernando were already exchanging pleasantries, it seemed like it would just be an act of meanness to do so. Especially since Leah looked so happy.

It was nice that Leah had found a man she could trust after her disastrous first marriage. Her husband had become addicted to painkillers after a skiing accident then died of a drug overdose, leaving Leah and her children destitute.

Even their sister, Erin, who also had a terrible first marriage, seemed to believe that love was possible again. Nicole wasn't so sure.

As Shane and Fernando talked, Leah led her into the other room.

"I'm sorry if this seems presumptuous, and maybe it isn't the right thing. But I'm really worried about you and the horse. Is there something else that happened with Fernando you haven't told me? I've always thought that you've treated him unfairly and were punishing him unjustly. Like I said earlier, I think it would be good for both of you to spend some time together and deal with your mutual grief."

She smiled at her sister. "I've dealt with my grief. I'm fine. I just don't need the constant reminders of my perfect life falling apart and having no clue."

She glanced in the direction of the kitchen, noting

that Fernando and Shane appeared to be in a very deep conversation. Like they were getting along. But that was the trouble. Great that they were friends. But did anyone think about what it meant to her?

What did Fernando think he had to gain in this situation? If he felt so bad about his sister's cheating, then why hadn't he just told her to begin with? Why had he let her be played for a fool, when apparently everyone else seemed to know? Her family hadn't, but they'd been dealing with their own stuff.

Every time she thought she was over it, Fernando had to step in and remind her. Even worse, he'd just shown her that the one thing that had been bringing her comfort after everything—working with this horse—was just one more mistake she'd made.

The men walked out of the kitchen, and she pasted a smile on her face.

"He's good," Shane said. "I'm really impressed with his horse knowledge. You'd be blessed to get a trainer like him. He's promised that he'll work with you and teach you. You'll still do most of the training yourself, but with his guidance."

Then his gaze landed firmly on Nicole. "I stand by what I said the other day. Unless Snookie gets proper training, she has to go."

Even though Shane had told her this before, it felt like the knife was being driven in even deeper.

"I'm sorry, Nicole," Shane said gently, looking at her like he did the boys when he was trying to be compassionate. "This is why I warned you not to fall in love with an animal just because it was pretty. I told you not to buy her, so now that you've got her, you need to do the right thing. Get her properly trained or give her to someone who can handle her."

She knew what he was referring to. The Springs Haven Animal Rescue was just a few miles outside the other end of town. They provided homes for abused and neglected animals, as well as animals that were surrendered by owners who could no longer care for them. She'd vowed not to be that kind of owner, someone who promised a home to an animal, then gave it up when the going got rough. Besides, at the last fund-raiser for the animal rescue, Margaret Cooke, the owner, had told people that she wasn't sure she'd have the funding to keep it going much longer. If the rescue closed, what would happen to Snookie? Shane looked regretful at reminding her of that option, but she knew that the boys' safety was his primary concern.

Fernando gave her a smile. "All is not lost. I think she's a good horse, very smart. But she's scared. Even though you're doing your best by her, your actions are making her more fearful because they're inconsistent with her nature."

Her fault. Wow. So much for thinking she could do the right thing.

But before she could even process the thought, Fernando stepped into her space and spoke quietly. "Don't be hard on yourself. You meant well, and most people would've made the same mistakes you have."

She nodded slowly, fighting the tears. This horse was supposed to help her, and she was supposed to help it. And together, they were going to help each other.

He touched her arm lightly. "Let me help you help

this horse. I believe you can do it. I know there is love in your heart for her, so let's get her to see it, too."

The last thing she ever wanted in her life was to have Fernando here. To have Fernando be a part of the peace she'd so carefully built around her heart.

But as she looked out at the barn, she knew she didn't have a choice. Her last hope, her only hope, was this man. She didn't like it, but how could she let this beautiful horse down?

Even though she'd already decided to let Fernando help her, she knew everyone else thought she was being difficult and needed convincing. But they didn't understand the emotional cost of admitting out loud that someone she held partially responsible for her pain was the right person to help her horse.

Fernando hated the way Nicole looked at him. Like he'd just taken a whip to poor Snookie himself.

But she had to understand the importance of the situation. Of doing the right thing by this horse.

"All right," Nicole said. "You can help with my horse."

Her tone was like that of someone agreeing to a root canal. But at least it meant he could stick around for a while. Figure out what happened to the woman who'd lost the light he'd once seen shining in her eyes.

Horses had saved him from a very dark period in his life. Maybe, if Nicole had the same chance he was given, she could find a new reason to be happy. A new reason to smile again, and not have it look like it caused her pain to contort her face in such a way.

The door opened, and Nicole's sister Erin walked in, followed by Leah's two sons, Dylan and Ryan.

"Fernando," Erin said, smiling in the fake way Nicole had been doing. "What brings you here?"

"I'm going to help Nicole train Snookie," he said. Nicole could fill her in on the rest. By the way Erin looked at him, it was clear she shared Nicole's anger at him.

"I see," Erin said. "Boys, why don't you get cleaned up for supper, then we can tell your mom all about what you saw at Mr. Ricky's."

The two boys raced past him, barely acknowledging him. He turned and watched them leave, appreciating their zest for life.

Fernando had once hoped to have a family of his own. But who would marry someone who'd been to prison? When he'd been arrested, Destiny, his fiancée, had told him she'd stand by him. But once they realized that the authorities were going to make an example of him, she'd slowly pulled away. Until she finally confessed she was embarrassed to admit he was in prison and didn't want her future children to face the same stigma. Every time he dated a woman and that fact came out, she lost interest.

Still, it bothered him to think that some of his most treasured dreams would never come true.

"Don't get any ideas," Nicole said, coming up behind him. "Even if you manage to befriend the rest of my family, you and I are never going to be friends."

"That's kind of harsh, don't you think?" Shane stepped forward. "I know you're mad at Fernando for keeping things secret from you, but maybe you should give him the chance to explain, to see things from his side."

Leah put her arm around Shane's waist. "Exactly. I don't think it was right for Fernando to not tell you about Adriana's affair with Brandon, but having seen him with Snookie, and how hard he's trying to do the right thing here, I have to believe that there's more to the story. Give him a chance."

Instead of Leah's words being encouraging to Nicole, they only seemed to make Nicole's face scrunch up, like she was trying not to tell Leah exactly what she thought of her sisterly advice. But then, just as quickly as the anger filled her face, the fake smile returned.

"I'm letting him train my horse, aren't I? As for why, I don't care. I just want to get my horse trained, and then both Fernando and I can move on with our lives. Separately."

Fine by him. It wasn't like he and Nicole had a future together. And the more she reminded him of it, the less tempted he was to wish his life were different.

"Whatever you want," Fernando said. "I'm only trying to help. I'd leave now, except that I want to work with Snookie. Can we call a temporary truce for her sake?"

Crazy to think that a horse would be the thing they could find common ground on.

"Fine." Nicole turned and glared at Leah. "But don't think this means anything."

Leah was obviously happy with Shane, and from what he knew of Leah losing her first husband, Fernando was glad to see her get a second chance at love. Hopefully, Leah's example would show Nicole that not all men were like Brandon, and that she, too, could find happiness.

Except, instead of that thought making Fernando feel good for Nicole, it made his heart hurt a little bit at the thought of her with anyone else. Crazy, since he couldn't have her for himself. He wanted her to be happy. And he prayed for the man who could do it.

Shane cleared his throat. "There's also the small item of payment. While you said you were happy to do it for free, it wouldn't be right for us to not pay you."

Not this again. They'd already argued about it in the kitchen, and Fernando thought it was the end of things. But obviously, Shane had another plan. Which, by the expression on Nicole's and her sisters' faces, was exactly where this conversation was going.

"I agree," Erin said. "We've budgeted for horse training."

Then Erin sighed. "Probably not what you're used to getting, but…"

"I'm not used to being paid for working with horses," Fernando said. "I do construction for a living."

Nicole gave him a funny look. "That's right, you do. Why are you going to Salida? Isn't that where your creepy uncle lives? Adriana once told me that you wouldn't work for him for a million dollars."

That was when he had a good job and he thought they valued him, despite his record.

"I got laid off," he said quietly, grateful they'd at least done that for him. The uncomfortable silence made him wish he hadn't said anything, but he didn't want to lie, either.

Finally, Shane said, "Training Snookie isn't going

to be a full-time job for you. Since you're in construction, maybe you could help with some of the things around here. I've been doing what I can, but with my own ranch, I can't do as much as I'd like."

"Yes," Leah added. "We also have money in the budget to pay for some of the repairs, but getting anyone to come out here is really tough."

He studied Nicole's face, trying to gauge her reaction. She already didn't want him here.

"It would keep him out of my hair," she said.

There were worse answers, he supposed.

"And we still haven't gotten that chicken coop fixed," Erin added. "It's too smelly to breathe in there."

Nicole giggled. "So basically, give him all the stuff we don't want to do?"

If she thought cleaning up a bunch of chicken manure was going to scare him away, she obviously hadn't heard enough stories about his uncle from Adriana. The only stories Adriana probably hadn't told Nicole were the ones about him. His entire family was ashamed of his time in prison, and all they ever told anyone about his seven-year absence was that he was off finding himself.

He had found himself. In a lot of unexpected ways. It just hadn't been the youthful lark everyone made it sound like. He might have been young and stupid, but at eighteen, he'd been legally an adult and paid adult consequences.

"I'd be happy to," Fernando said. "I can tell this place needs some improvements, and I'm familiar with the work. It won't be a problem. Just give me a list, and I'll take care of it."

They discussed his wage, and while it was more

than reasonable, Fernando couldn't help wishing they'd found a way to disagree. But he couldn't, in all fairness, ask for more, which would have been the only way they wouldn't have come to an agreement.

Shane looked over at Fernando. "Why don't you come with me? Leah and I were talking about the apartment over the barn. I stayed there when I first came to Columbine Springs years ago, and it hasn't been used since. We were going to fix it up as guest quarters."

He looked apologetic, but then shrugged. "It needs some work, but it's habitable."

Fernando nodded at the man's thoughtfulness, but he looked over at Nicole to see how she felt about the idea. Her face was expressionless, which was a good sign, considering the hostility she'd once had toward him.

"Thanks. I was going to go look for a hotel or something. But if it's not too much of an imposition, that would be great."

Shane chuckled. "There isn't much in Columbine Springs. We had some city folks try to establish a B&B, but they didn't last long. There was an old hotel, but it's been closed now for at least ten years."

He liked Shane. He hoped they could be friends, but just as he had the idea, he dismissed it as being stupid. He didn't want to establish ties here if it would cause Nicole more pain. Yes, she had to deal with her grief. But he knew he was walking a fine line, and he wasn't going to insert himself into her life any further than was healthy for her.

Or for him.

It wasn't just Adriana's actions he didn't understand but Brandon's. Despite her obvious faults, his sister had been a great person, but in a way, Nicole was even better. She represented everything he wanted in a woman. She was smart, funny, kind to children and animals, and she had a zest for living that had always inspired him. How could Brandon have treated her so badly?

Maybe that's why he'd been trying so hard to help Nicole. He'd always admired her, and seeing how bitter she'd become bothered him.

No, he didn't think he stood a chance at her heart. No woman should be stuck with a guy like him. As an ex-con, he couldn't give any woman the kind of life she deserved. Especially someone as wonderful as Nicole.

Or at least as Nicole had been.

Was that woman still inside?

As Shane led him out to the barn, Snookie neighed, reminding him of the other reason he was here.

Snookie was where he had to stay focused. He could help the horse. Nicole—that was something he had to leave alone.

Chapter Three

Nicole went into the small apartment above the barn, carrying some linens Leah had asked her to bring over for Fernando. After everything that had been said earlier, she didn't really want to talk to him, but her sisters had made it clear she had to stop running from the pain. She still wasn't sure what to say to him.

The apartment wasn't what you would call luxury lodgings, but Fernando had said he didn't mind and had even promised to help fix it up. Which made Nicole feel like even more of a jerk for not welcoming him with open arms. He'd done everything he could to be nice, and she kept shoving him away.

But how did one welcome the reminder of your biggest mistakes with joy? He didn't answer her knock on the door, and she remembered hearing that he'd wanted to take a walk later. When she let herself in, she saw him sound asleep, sprawled out on the bare mattress. She looked down at the bundle of sheets and blankets she'd brought. Moving as quietly as possible, she carried them to the dresser. But as she set them on top, Fernando yelled, "I didn't do it! Leave me be."

She turned, but Fernando was still fast asleep, tossing and turning on the bed.

"I didn't tell. It wasn't me! I promise, I didn't help."

He was having a bad dream. And from the way he thrashed about, it was a terrible one.

"Please. I beg you. Don't do this. It wasn't me."

Should she wake him? She took a step toward him, and the board creaked.

Fernando sat bolt upright. "What?"

He seemed wide awake now.

"I'm sorry. I didn't mean to wake you. I just brought you some linens."

He nodded slowly as he looked around the room.

"It's all right," she told him, wanting to comfort him like she did her nephews when they had nightmares, but not feeling so generous as to want to give him a cuddle the way she did with the boys.

Then he looked at her more closely. "You look like you just saw something terrifying. Was I talking in my sleep again?"

Nicole nodded slowly. "I wasn't afraid of you, though. I was afraid for you. It seemed like you were having the most awful dream."

He ran his fingers through his hair as he nodded. "*Sí.* I mean, yes. What did I say?"

He looked so out of sorts, it seemed almost impossible to withhold compassion.

She walked over and sat on the edge of the bad, near him, but not next to him. "You can use Spanish around

me if you want. Adriana did sometimes, and she was
trying to teach me a few words."

Then she shook her head. "I don't know why I just
said that. That was dumb of me."

Especially the part about Adriana. She'd done her
best to forget about her former best friend, and it was
weird the way the memory came back up so quickly.
Part of why she hadn't wanted Fernando around in the
first place. She didn't need the reminders. But he was
here now, and she had to deal with it.

He shook his head slowly. "Thanks. I don't…"

Fernando seemed unsure of himself, hesitant. And
she didn't blame him. After all, she'd done everything
she could to make him feel unwelcome, and now that
he was clearly in the middle of something disturbing,
he wouldn't find her very comforting. And honestly,
she wasn't sure she wanted to be that person for him.

"I'm sorry." She stood, then gestured at the blankets.
"I was going to try to soothe you or something, but I
can't imagine that you would feel comforted by me. I
haven't been very nice to you, and I don't exactly have
warm feelings toward you."

Even as the admission came out, she knew there was
one more thing she had to do. Not that she liked it much.

"My sisters say I owe you an apology," she said.

"But you disagree." There was no judgment in his
voice, no anger. Just acceptance.

She shrugged. "Obviously."

He nodded slowly as he yawned, then ran his hands
over his face.

"Sorry. I guess I was more tired than I thought." He
stood, then came next to her. "Listen. You don't owe

me anything. But we do have to get to a place where we can stop rehashing the fact that you're angry with me for not telling you about Adriana and Brandon and move forward to a place of understanding. I know forgiveness is hard, and I'm not asking you to do it right away. But it has to happen at some point, even if only for your own peace of mind. You know the quote about unforgiveness being like drinking poison while waiting for the other person to die?"

Factually, she knew all of this to be true. It wasn't like she didn't know that she was only hurting herself by not forgiving him. That God wanted her to forgive him. But there was so much injustice in the situation, and it didn't seem right that no one had been held accountable to her for their actions.

"I get that. I do, I promise." He'd been nothing but nice to her. Even Leah, who had always been angry on her behalf, was warming to him because of how nice he was.

"You just have to understand," Nicole said. "I didn't find out until I was on my way to the church to be married. The perfect man, the perfect friend, all at once, they were lost to me. And they died before I could even ask them why. Before I could confront them and tell them what a terrible thing it was that they did to me."

"So you took it out on me instead."

"It's all I had."

Her confession was more cathartic than she'd thought it would be. But she still needed answers.

"Even though we sort of agreed not to rehash this, in all the apologies you've given me, you've never told me why. Why didn't you tell me about Adriana and Brandon?"

He looked down at the ground, then back up at her. "I didn't think it was my place. I talked to Adriana, and I tried convincing her to do the right thing. If it's any consolation, I don't think she meant to hurt you. I think that's why she wouldn't tell you."

He let out a long sigh, and for the first time, she recognized the torment on his face.

"Your niece had recently died, and so shortly after your brother-in-law's death. Adriana told me that she didn't think you would be able to handle it. She asked me to trust her. That she would take care of things, but I needed to be patient. I didn't know what that meant. But where I come from, you stay out of other people's business. Trust me when I say that butting in has cost me a lot in my life."

She looked down at the ground, then back up at him.

Because she'd always refused to meet him, or even talk to him about this, she'd never seen this look of regret on his face. Never heard the pain in his voice.

All the times she'd hung up on him, refused to take his calls, raged against him, she'd missed seeing his level of brokenness. She'd never realized that as much as she had been hurting, he had been hurting, too.

Suddenly, Fernando's decision to keep Adriana's secret didn't seem so awful. Just really unfair that she had to be the victim.

"I get it," Nicole said. "You were caught in the middle. Between someone you loved and doing the right thing."

He nodded slowly. "Keeping secrets is a terrible burden, but so is knowing who and what to tell. My only hope is that in time, you can forgive me, forgive them, and move on with your life."

It should be easy for her to just say, "I forgive you," but it wasn't that simple. She could say the words, but she was a long way from feeling that peace in her heart.

"I'm not there yet," she said, hoping that honesty was the best policy here. Of all the things she'd wished since she'd found out about Brandon and Adriana, her greatest desire had been for people to just be honest with her. It seemed like everyone danced around the truth, afraid of hurting people. And maybe the truth did hurt sometimes, but it always came out, and it seemed to hurt far more having it hidden so long.

"They make it sound easy in church, don't they?" Fernando looked at her sympathetically, like it didn't bother him to hear forgiveness wasn't going to come easily. But considering she'd told him she'd hate him forever several times, he probably wasn't expecting even this.

She nodded. "Yeah. And even though Jesus tells us that we should forgive seventy times seven, I'm really struggling with just once. But it makes me feel good to know that you're willing to be patient with the process."

Even that was a breakthrough for her, considering that until now, she hadn't wanted to forgive him.

He walked over to the dresser and picked up the sheets. "Thank you for bringing these. And thank you for letting me stay. If there were any hotels in town, I'd have stayed there."

"Nearest one is about thirty minutes down the road. But I wouldn't let my worst enemy stay there."

He gave her a smile that made her tingle down to the very bottom of her toes. "Well, at least I have that going for me. You don't like me, but I'm not your worst enemy."

The few times that she'd met Fernando when he was with his sister, she'd thought he had a nice sense of humor, a good smile, and was a lot of fun to be around. She'd liked him even then, and had, for a brief period, thought they were friends. But either she had been mistaken in her beliefs about him, or neither one of them understood what friendship really was.

Still, it was weird, feeling this warming toward him. It wasn't just the sympathy she'd felt for him upon coming to see him in the room; it was almost like attraction. But that was crazy. She couldn't be, wouldn't be, attracted to someone who'd done so much damage in her life.

Fernando unfolded one of the sheets. "Can you take the other end and help me?"

When she reached to take the end of the sheet out of his hands, her fingers brushed his, and she felt that same weird jolt she had earlier with the horse. She jumped slightly, and Fernando looked at her.

"Static electricity," she said. It had to be. There couldn't be any other explanation.

She turned to Fernando and smiled as she smoothed the sheet over her side of the bed. "So that nightmare. It seemed pretty bad. Do you have it often?"

Fernando kept his attention on the bed. "Often enough. Nothing to worry about. Thank you for asking. Why don't you tell me about the ranch, why you're here, your plans for it?"

* * *

When Nicole launched into the story of inheriting a ranch from her former stepmother, Fernando breathed a sigh of relief. Though part of him appreciated Nicole's compassion and the indication of her softening toward him, deep inside, he was shaking.

They'd just gotten to a place where she was beginning to warm to the idea of forgiving him. How would that change when she knew about his past, which was what he'd been dreaming about?

He was so tired of the inevitable rejection that came with his admission of having gone to prison. No one looked at him the same, and no matter what he said in his defense, people shut down at the word *felon*.

He took a deep breath and focused on Nicole as she spoke. The light in her that he remembered from before her failed wedding had returned, and he couldn't help thinking about what a beautiful woman she was.

Even though the apartment above the barn had plenty of windows, suddenly the space felt too confining. It wasn't good for him to sit here, thinking about all the things he liked about her.

"Why don't you show me around," he said, standing and holding his hand out to her.

Nicole stood but didn't take his hand. He hadn't expected her to, but it had seemed right to make the gesture. She led him outside.

It felt good to be out in the open air, where he could breathe. That was one of the things he'd loved about being in the horse training program in prison. The chance to be outside, in nature, with horses.

He followed Nicole to a run-down chicken coop.

"I really want chickens," she said. "We got some when we first came, but the coop isn't very secure, and a fox got in. Plus, Shane says that we should clean it out in case of disease."

As he entered the coop, he pulled his shirt over his nose. Erin hadn't been joking about the place being smelly. He could definitely see why Shane wanted it cleaned out before getting more chickens.

"It sounds like Shane has been really helpful," he said.

"I know I sounded cranky about him earlier, so I should apologize. I have nothing against Shane. He's wonderful, and he has been a big help. But more than that, he makes my sister happy, and the boys love him."

Nicole kicked a rock. "I guess I'm just frustrated sometimes that this was supposed to be our adventure—mine and my sisters'—and then Leah had to go and fall in love. I'm happy for her, but I really was looking forward to the three of us rebuilding the ranch."

After latching the coop back up to prevent anything else from getting in, Fernando turned to her. "But maybe that is the adventure. Bringing new people into your lives to share it with."

He gestured around at the property in general. "This is so big, I can't imagine anyone doing it alone. It's good that you have help. Why are you fighting it?"

Nicole shrugged, then shook her head. "I don't know. It was probably stupid of me to say anything. Let me show you where I want to put the goats."

Once again, she was shutting down and shutting him out. Part of him regretted saying anything, except that it gave him another peek into her heart. It was like she was afraid of being vulnerable, and in some ways, he didn't blame her.

As he followed her, he made note of the other things that were in need of repair. He'd put together his own list, then talk to the family about it. Based on what Nicole had said about being unprepared for chickens, and as well as her decision to buy a horse against Shane's advice, he was fairly certain that they would need help prioritizing projects.

"It's great that you have so many plans," he said when they finally stopped at a large, ramshackle barn. "I remember you saying that you've always wanted animals, but I never saw you as the type to move to a ranch in the middle of nowhere."

The smile she gave him was warm and genuine. "When I was a kid, I used to always play farm. But because we moved around so much for the Colonel's job, it wasn't practical to have pets. Then real life happened, and still, no animals. I managed to have a few in my preschool classroom—fish, hamsters, even a snake once. But I'll admit that our field trips to the petting zoo were more fun for me than they were for the kids."

"The Colonel? Who is that?" He thought he knew about Nicole's family, but he hadn't heard mention of the Colonel before.

"Our father." Nicole let out a long sigh. "He was in the military and ran his household like it. We were his troops, not his children, and we took to referring to him as the Colonel when we got older. I know that sounds disrespectful, but he wasn't much of a father."

He reached out to touch her arm in comfort, but she jerked away.

"I don't want your pity. It's fine. My sisters and I accepted long ago that we were all each other had. I know you think you're trying to be there for me, but I have them, and that's all I need."

And yet, she did need him. At least for her horse.

"I'm sure you can take care of yourself, but it doesn't make you weak to let others in," Fernando said.

"Maybe not," she admitted. "But I spent most of my life knowing that the only people I could count on were my sisters. And the first time I took a risk in trusting someone new, I found myself burned beyond recognition."

She reached forward and touched his arm gently. "I can tell you want to help, and I appreciate the gesture. I'm grateful that you're willing to train my horse. I'm also grateful that you're willing to help fix things around here. We tried hiring laborers, but it's hard to compete with the larger ranches who can pay more."

He knew the *but* was coming even before the expression hit her face and the words left her mouth.

"But that's all I want from you. I got the answers I needed. You don't owe me anything else. So please stop trying to be my friend and asking me questions beyond what you need to know to do your job."

Nicole's brow furrowed, like she realized that she'd been a little too harsh with him.

"It's just too confusing for me right now to talk about personal things," she finally said. "I don't like this angry version of myself, but when I'm around you, I can't help it. I let my guard down, and then I remember that I'm still mad at you, even though I'm trying to get past it. The emotions that take over are hard for me to handle. I'm sorry."

Her admission made him realize that maybe he'd been pushing her too hard. All this time, his need for her to forgive him was all about him making things right. Even though he'd assumed that the right thing for Nicole was to let go of the past, he hadn't taken the time to understand her actual needs. He'd assumed a lot on her behalf, starting with when he'd decided to keep Adriana's secret from her, continuing to now.

"It's okay," Fernando said. "I know I've been pushing you hard. You've been asking me for space, and I haven't given it to you. I'm sorry. I'll do better in the future."

She nodded slowly, and he could see her posture relax slightly.

He gestured to the barn they'd stopped in front of. "Do you want to tell me about your plans for this? I assume it was used to store hay and other equipment in the past, but it looks like it's in need of a lot of TLC."

The rest of her resistance melted away as she led him to the entrance. "Shane says the bones are still strong, but it does need a lot of repairs. My sisters and I were thinking we could use it as an event center, like for destination weddings or something. Ricky, our neighbor at the Double R, has a dude ranch, but he doesn't have a facility his guests can use for their events. This would help both of our businesses grow."

As Nicole explained their plans for the barn, Fernando could see where, of all the projects, this would be the one that would provide the best long-term benefit.

"I like your plans a lot," Fernando said when she finally finished. "If you don't mind, I'm going to take a better look at everything and I'll come up with a list. Then you and your sisters can tell me what your priorities are and where you can best use me."

The look she gave him was less grudging than she'd been with him in the past. Even though they'd been in two totally different situations, he could almost relate. Until this point, he'd taken the control of their relationship away from her. He'd kept valuable information about her fiancé and best friend from her. He'd continued contacting her when she'd asked him to give her space. He'd forced her hand with Snookie. Now, she had a choice.

Whatever she decided, Fernando was going to respect it.

Chapter Four

The trouble with holding a grudge against someone for so long was that having Fernando in her life felt awkward. Nicole had spent so many hours, days, weeks, months, wanting him to feel as horrible as she did. But as she watched Fernando in the round pen with Snookie, she didn't feel better, knowing how bad he felt. She was the horrible one. He'd been nothing but nice to her, reaching out to her in compassion and apologizing for his mistakes.

Though they'd technically cleared the air between them, watching him work with Snookie only made her feel worse about how she'd treated him when he first arrived. The previous trainer they'd talked to about her had wanted double what they were paying Fernando. And Fernando was way more skilled than the other trainer had been. So the question was, if Fernando was so good with horses, why was he wasting his time on a job with his uncle when he could clearly do better elsewhere?

The answers to those questions were none of her

business. She wasn't supposed to care about Fernando or his situation. It shouldn't matter to her what kind of job he did or if he could pursue his passion.

Snookie reared, nearly knocking Fernando off-balance. But he quickly righted himself and gave the horse a small correction. She liked the gentleness that Fernando always used, and even though it was supposed to be making the horse feel safe, it also calmed something in Nicole's heart.

She'd have liked to have said something friendly and encouraging in response to his skill, but she didn't want to get too personal or make him think that she was open to anything other than a working relationship.

"Lunch is ready," Erin said, coming to stand beside her. "You should see if Fernando is hungry."

It was a rare day when both sisters were off at the same time. Leah stayed home to manage their ranch and take care of her sons, but also helped with Shane's ranch from time to time.

Erin worked as an accountant for a neighboring dude ranch, the Double R. With as little as Three Sisters Ranch was bringing in, it made sense for Erin to use her accounting skills at another ranch where she could learn that end of the business and be useful for when theirs was profitable.

The sisters were slowly discovering that they still had a lot to learn before their ranch would provide them with a livable income, which was why having the big barn for events would be good for their family. It seemed like for a ranch to be profitable these days, it needed more than one source of income.

Approaching Fernando, Nicole said, "She's looking good."

Fernando guided the horse toward her, stopping nearby. "What's up?"

"Lunch is ready," she said.

Fernando patted the horse. "We're not at a good stopping point yet. I'll grab something later."

Though Snookie was grudgingly obeying his commands, Nicole could see by the set of the horse's body and the way she pinned her ears back that she wasn't doing it willingly. The goal in training a horse was to make them want to do the work. So many people forced the issue, getting a horse's obedience but not the respect.

Based on what she'd studied, a horse who couldn't yield with respect was dangerous, because at some point, that horse would get sick of being told what to do and would do whatever it wanted. People forgot that horses were still wild and made their own decisions.

Unexpectedly, tears filled her eyes at the thought of the wildness of a horse who didn't respect the people around it. Was she any different?

Fernando brought Snookie back to where he'd been working with her and returned to work.

The trouble with having Fernando here was that she was starting to look at the past in a more analytical way, rather than trying to pretend it never happened. Because of Fernando, she was being forced to deal with things she'd been trying to ignore.

Erin stepped beside her and put her arm around her. "Are you okay? You look upset."

Nicole looked over her sister. "I'm watching Fernando train the horse and thinking that we aren't so different, Snookie and me. I was so stubborn about my wedding, wanting my own way. Even though Brandon never said he didn't want to marry me, he suggested that we postpone a number of times. I never looked at it from his perspective or asked deeper questions about what he really wanted. It was all about me."

Erin gave her a squeeze. "It doesn't justify his actions."

"No, it doesn't," Nicole said. "But for the first time, instead of making it all his fault, I'm wondering what my part in all of it was. I can be just as stubborn as Snookie. I spend so much time focused on my needs and what I want that I don't always see others' needs."

Erin chuckled. "Welcome to being human. Don't beat yourself up. We all do it. There's nothing you can do, given that we're talking about a dead man who can't give you the answers you need. All you can do is look forward and decide to do better in future relationships."

Nicole looked over at her sister, who wore a thoughtful expression. "You're thinking about Lance, aren't you?" Nicole asked.

Erin shrugged. "Like you, I'm prone to my moments of melancholy. Sometimes I wonder if ending my marriage to Lance was the right thing to do. I still love him, but what was happening between us wasn't healthy, and I couldn't handle the constant fighting over things that would never be solved. Our daughter was dead, and I thought having each other would be enough, but I was wrong."

Erin reached up and fingered the locket she always wore. It contained Lily's baby picture, along with a lock of her hair.

Nicole put her arms around her sister, and Erin rested her head on Nicole's shoulder. "I just have to hold on to God's goodness," Erin said. "Even though it sometimes feels like my life has ended, my story isn't over. There's still a chance for wonderful things to come my way."

Then Erin looked up at Nicole. "I believe that for you, too."

Some of the heaviness in Nicole's heart lifted, and as she looked over at Fernando working with Snookie, she realized that she'd been holding back from living because she'd been so buried in the resentment of broken dreams.

Sure, she'd been focused on building the ranch with her sisters, but she'd also spent a lot of her energy on hating Fernando.

And for what?

It didn't change anything in her past, and it certainly hadn't helped her future. But letting go of her resentment of Fernando just might.

Maybe he'd been right that holding on to her unforgiveness was hurting more than it was helping her.

She turned and gave Erin another hug. "I know it's hard for you to talk about your losses, but it really means a lot to me. It makes me feel not so alone."

Erin hugged her back. "It helped me as much as it helped you." Then Erin gestured at Fernando. "I know you don't want him here, because it reminds you of your pain. When Lily first died, it was hard being around the boys. Especially because she and Ryan had been so close. But then I realized how much he missed her, and helping him helped me."

With a loving look on her face, Erin turned her attention back to Nicole. "Even though Fernando says he's here to help us, maybe we need to help him, too. Sharing my pain was the only way I got through my grief. Maybe it's time for you to do the same."

Erin's words were like a sharp kick in the stomach. Nicole's immediate response was that she wanted to ask her sister whose side she was on. But as she saw the genuine compassion in Erin's eyes, she had to wonder if maybe Erin and Leah were right. This whole time, Nicole had been selfishly thinking about the pain she carried, but not what anyone else, especially Fernando, had been enduring.

And as she watched him tirelessly going through the same motions designed to break down the barriers around Snookie's heart, she wondered if maybe it was time to let some of her own down as well.

The horse was proving to be more stubborn than Fernando initially thought. But that was a mare for you. Finally, she showed enough signs of submission that he thought they might be getting somewhere.

"Good girl," he said, giving her a pat. He rode her over to the gate, where Nicole and Erin were watching.

He knew Nicole probably wanted to get the training over with so that he could be out of her hair forever. But horses didn't work on a timeline, especially not this one. Snookie had to be the most stubborn mare he'd ever worked with.

Nicole, with her tender heart, would obviously want to help a horse like Snookie. But Snookie wasn't a starter horse, and her issues were challenging, even for him.

He pulled off his hat and wiped his brow. He hadn't realized how late it had gotten.

Erin handed him a bottle of water. "You've been working hard," she said. "Lunch has been ready for a while, but I'll admit I've enjoyed watching the horse in action."

He took a long drink of water, grateful for refreshment. "Nicole told me. I wasn't expecting you to wait on me."

He looked at Nicole, and she gave the same nonchalant shrug she always did whenever he tried including her. She might have said she accepted him being there, but her grudging attitude spoke louder.

"I meant to go back in," Nicole said. "But, like Erin, I got caught up watching."

She reached forward and patted the horse. "You did good."

Was she talking about him or the horse? Fernando didn't know and he wasn't going to ask.

"I think she's slowly getting there," Fernando said. "It just takes patience."

Nicole smiled at him. "And you seem to have a great deal of it. She's stubborn, and I haven't seen you lose your temper at all."

He grinned and took another drink of his water before answering. "Trust me, there have been times I've wanted to. But it serves no purpose. She doesn't understand if I yell at her. Yelling just makes her think I'm a big scary human and that she's in danger. The key is to be calm at all times and not let your emotions get the better of you."

Nicole nodded intelligently—based on what she'd

mentioned watching and reading, these concepts were likely familiar to her. But he saw an even deeper connection, one she might not understand.

"I believe horses can sense what we're feeling," he continued. "They feed off our energy. If we stand before them, frustrated and upset, they may not understand it, but they sense something is amiss. So they act on it. If a horse is frightened or upset, the last thing they need is for us to continue feeding that emotion."

He liked that Nicole seemed to take his words in, a thoughtful expression on her face.

"I saw a show once," Nicole said. "Where the people in the demonstration were supposed to think positive thoughts and the horse would come to them. Then they would think negative thoughts and see what the horse would do. The people who said they were thinking positive thoughts, the horse always ended up following them around. But for the people with negative thoughts, it was harder to get to the horse to behave."

Fernando nodded. "I've seen that, too. I went to one of those trainings."

Erin groaned. "All right, horse nerds. I'm out. No offense, but Nicole has spent hours making us watch those boring videos, and while I appreciate where you're coming from, lunch is far more interesting to me. I'm hungry."

He chuckled and watched as Erin turned to go back to the house. He half expected Nicole to follow, but instead, she turned to him.

"Did you find the training useful?" Nicole asked.

The answer to her question was treading a delicate line. The trainer had come to the prison, not just to help the men learn how to work with their horses, but also to teach them how to control their emotions. To see the impact their emotions had on others.

It had probably been the most valuable lesson he'd learned. One he needed to remember here with Nicole. She was just as skittish as a newly caught horse.

"I did," he said slowly, weighing what to tell her that would be helpful versus what would reveal too much about his past.

She gave Snookie another pat. "Do you use that technique with her?"

Nicole's question and the curiosity in her eyes demonstrated an openness to him that he hadn't seen in her before. For the first time, she didn't appear to be conversing with him out of a grudging acceptance that he had to be there.

Was there hope that they could get along after all?

"Yes," he said. "It sounds crazy, but every time I work with a horse, I always pray and ask God to give me guidance on how to bond with the horse. As God's creatures, I think the horses sense God's love within me and know that my actions toward them stem from God's love."

Nicole murmured and nodded, like his words made sense to her. Once again, he couldn't help thinking how much he admired her. Working with the horses wasn't the only area in which he needed God to give him strength.

"When I'm frustrated with the horse," he continued, "I can draw on the love of God to keep me calm and peaceful, using God's strength to be what the horse needs."

Nicole smiled at him. "I hadn't thought of it that way. But you're right. God's love is stronger than anything we have on our own. I think about all the things I try to do on my own strength and—"

She shook her head slowly, appearing deep in thought. "I can't believe I never thought to ask for God's help."

Watching the different expressions cross her face almost made him feel like he was intruding on a private conversation between her and God. But as he took a deep breath and silently asked God what he was supposed to do in this situation, he realized he already had the answer.

Maybe, if Nicole could open her heart to God in working with Snookie, Nicole would let God work in other areas of her life as well.

Perhaps that was the real reason God had brought Fernando here. The horse had just been the excuse for the greater work God wanted to do in Nicole's heart.

Snookie nudged him softly as if to confirm his thoughts.

He gave the horse a pat and turned back to Nicole. "It's funny how complicated we make things when we forget to consult the Lord."

Nicole groaned. "I know. I didn't listen when Shane said not to get Snookie. And I sure didn't ask God. I wanted a horse so bad, and I really thought Snookie was speaking to me. Telling me we belonged together."

Then Nicole shook her head slowly. "But that was just wishful thinking, wasn't it? It was just those long-held dreams, tired of being patient."

Fernando reached out and touched her arm gently.

"I don't know. It's possible that she did speak to you. And it's possible that you were too impatient in getting her. But God is capable of redeeming our mistakes, so there is hope for you and Snookie yet."

The smile she gave him warmed his heart. "Do you think so? I was just telling Erin how selfish I'd been in…" she shook her head. "It doesn't matter. But maybe I was selfish in wanting Snookie. Thinking of my needs, but not hers. Certainly not my family's."

She looked up at him with a mixture of sadness and desperation, and something in her eyes told him that she was earnestly trying to do the right thing.

Something he could help her with.

"I believe that horses, just like people, can be redeemed. Snookie just needs love and a bond with someone willing to love her. I won't be with her forever. But you will. As we train her, she'll bond to you and will feel safe once I'm gone."

Nicole's face lit up. "You don't think she's a danger to the boys?"

He shrugged. "I think she's got some bad habits, born mostly out of self-protection. But we can help her learn new ones, and we can help her feel safe. Do you want to try?"

Even though he was still holding the horse, Nicole threw her arms around him and gave him a hug.

"Thank you for not giving up on me," she said. "And thank you for giving me the opportunity to have a second chance with Snookie. You have no idea how much this means to me."

And even though Snookie usually reacted badly to

sudden movements, she seemed to sense the enormity of what had just happened and remained still.

Maybe it was his own foolishness, but it felt like, in this moment, God was giving them all a big hug, telling them everything would be okay. Fernando just wished he had that same feeling about the bigger picture of his life.

He'd prayed for a long time about what he was supposed to do, and it seemed like every door he'd hoped to walk through ended up being closed to him. Going to work for his uncle had seemed like the right decision, since it was the only open door, and he'd been praying for God to open the right doors, but deep in the pit of his stomach, Fernando was dreading the day when he'd walk onto his uncle's job site.

His body must have tensed at the thought, because Nicole pulled away. "I'm sorry. I hope I didn't make you uncomfortable with my hug. I know I haven't been very welcoming to you, but I really am trying. And, thanks to our conversation, I'll spend more time talking to God about all of this."

The shy smile she gave him brought more confidence to his plans. His stop in Columbine Springs was only meant to be a short visit, but clearly God had other plans. Who knew what plans God had for him in working a job he didn't want? He had to be open to whatever God's workings were.

"Don't be sorry," Fernando said. "It did me a lot of good. Funny, in all this time I've known you, I didn't realize you were a believer. I guess you're right that there's a lot I don't know about you. But I'm glad for this opportunity."

Nicole shrugged. "Back when you knew me, I wasn't much of one. But since moving here, we've become involved with the Columbine Springs Community Church. My faith has become very important to me."

Then she gave a tiny laugh as she pushed her hair off her face. "But, as you can see, I still have a lot to learn about leaning on God."

"We all do," he assured her. "Thank you for trusting me with your struggles. It's our job as brothers and sisters in Christ."

He just wished it was safe for him to trust someone with his struggles. His past. Adriana used to tease Nicole for being such a good girl that she wouldn't cross the street against the light even if there were no cars coming. How would she judge him for committing a real crime?

She looked pensive for a moment, then turned her gaze out across the fields before looking at him again. "I don't let a lot of people in. The closest are my sisters, but having you here has taught me how much I shut them out. I trusted Brandon and Adriana with everything, and look where that got me. Somewhere there has to be an in-between, but I don't know how to find it."

"Or you just trusted the wrong people," he said softly. He knew all about trusting the wrong people. After all, that's how he'd ended up ruining his life.

"Maybe," Nicole said. Then she looked over at the house. "I suppose I should stop chewing your ear off and let you get some lunch. You're probably hungry after all of your hard work."

She turned to leave, then stopped. "Oh, and you should come to church with us on Sunday. Our pastor talks about God a lot like you do. I think you'd like him."

Not waiting for an answer, she went into the house, skipping up the stairs of the back porch like whatever load she'd been carrying had been lightened. Clearly, their conversation had helped her.

But it had only left more uncertainty for him. He'd tried going to church, but as soon as he got involved and people found out about his record, they treated him differently, like they were afraid of him or what he might do. He'd moved to watching the sermons online, where he wouldn't have to walk through the sanctuary, listening to people whisper about him. The chaplain at the prison would have told him that he needed the actual fellowship of other believers, but so far Fernando hadn't found anyone willing to accept him when they found out what he'd done.

So what was he supposed to do with this invitation?

Chapter Five

Nicole craned her neck to see if Fernando had come into the church yet. They'd offered to let him ride with them to save on gas, but he'd said he had some errands to run in town, so he'd take his own vehicle. However, when they'd arrived at the church, Fernando hadn't gotten out of his truck.

The music was just starting, and so far, Fernando hadn't entered the sanctuary. Nicole had put her Bible beside her to save a spot for him, but maybe he didn't want to sit with her. She hadn't exactly done much to make him feel welcome.

It didn't take long for Nicole to become engrossed in her favorite worship songs. Even though she was standing in a group of people, the experience always ended up feeling like a very personal time with God. As she closed her eyes, praising God, she felt like a newer, stronger person.

Pastor Roberts's sermon was on trusting the Lord, and it was like he'd been peeking into her life over the past several days. One more reason she needed to rely on God more than she should her own wisdom. It was like Proverbs 3:5 had been written just for her. But that was the amazing way God worked sometimes.

She glanced over her shoulder and realized that sometime during the service, Fernando had entered and taken a seat in the back. He'd probably not wanted to disturb anyone by coming up front to sit with them. But at least he was here.

After church, Leah went to get the boys from the Sunday school classroom, and Nicole hurried over to where she'd seen Fernando sitting. He was gone. Since she didn't see him in the crowd of people that had gathered afterward, she went outside to see if she could get a better view. His truck was no longer parked in its spot.

"Hey, Nicole," Miranda Gray, one of the women from Bible study, greeted her warmly. "Some of the people in the singles group are going out for lunch to discuss the sermon and what it means to trust in the Lord while being single. We'd love it if you could join us."

Was there a polite way to say that she was trusting in the Lord to keep her single after her humiliating almost trip down the aisle? But then she remembered her recent conversations with Erin and Fernando. That mistake had been all about her trusting in herself and doing what she wanted without consulting the Lord.

Did God have someone for her?

Fernando instantly came to mind, which she immediately dismissed as being ridiculous. She'd spent every single day since her failed wedding loathing him. Which wasn't how she felt about him now. Now, it was more…complicated.

And even if God wanted her to open herself up to

the idea of a new relationship, there was still a part of her that feared even making a new friend. Would she get hurt again?

Nicole smiled at Miranda. "It sounds like a lot of fun, but I have things at the ranch I have to do. Maybe another time."

She hoped her refusal wasn't too rude. But she wasn't ready to jump back in to anything, even if it was just hanging out with a bunch of random people from church. She'd already been brave enough in joining the women's Bible study, but so far, she hadn't done much to socialize with any of them outside the classroom.

"Sure," Miranda said. "You guys are really getting that place into shape. I was just driving past the other day, and I noticed you're working on that old barn of yours. Erin says you're going to turn it into an event space."

Even though Nicole knew Miranda was just being friendly, it was hard, trying to have a conversation with someone she wasn't sure she wanted to get to know. Miranda was probably a very nice person, but...

Janie Roberts, the pastor's daughter, and another one of the women who often invited her to gatherings, joined them.

"Are you coming to lunch with us?" she asked.

Nicole felt like a jerk for shaking her head. But she'd already opened her heart more this past week than she'd done in over a year, and she wasn't sure it could bear the weight of doing more.

"I was really hoping you'd come," Miranda said. "Not only have we all been wanting to get to know you better, but I'd love to hear more about the plans for the barn."

Janie gave Nicole an understanding look. "We can be overwhelming sometimes, but I promise, everyone is great."

Could she feel any more like a jerk? They were trying so hard, had been since she'd first started going to church here, yet she couldn't bring herself to accept their invitations.

"Maybe another time," Nicole said. "Thanks for asking."

Not wanting to continue the awkward conversation, Nicole smiled. "I hope you all have a great lunch and a great discussion. I'll see you around."

As she turned to leave, Dylan ran up to her. "Look what I made!"

He held up a picture from his Sunday school class, and as he explained it, she reminded herself that she had a wonderful family, and that was all she needed.

When they got back to the ranch, Fernando's truck was in its usual spot, and he was hard at work on the barn. He'd even had time to change out of his Sunday clothes.

Which meant he'd lied about having errands. There was no way he'd have had time to run any kind of errand, get home, change clothes and be so into the task at hand.

Maybe Nicole was better off not trusting anyone. Sure, it was a white lie, but a lie was a lie, and even the lies people didn't think would hurt a person ended up being damaging. She should have known better than to trust him.

"How was your errand?" she asked as she walked up on him. Probably stupid to ask him something that would end up making him lie again, but part of her hoped that it would lead to him telling the truth.

Because why would anyone lie about having an errand to run to avoid having to ride with them to church when gas was so expensive?

Fernando hesitated. She squeezed her eyes shut as she tried to block out the image of all the times Brandon had done the same thing when she'd asked where he'd been. He'd been with Adriana and had needed a second to make up a lie. Obviously, Fernando wasn't cheating on Nicole, but it still didn't feel good to know he was lying to her.

"I didn't get the chance to take care of it," he finally said, looking around. "I needed something from the ranch store, and I forgot to bring measurements."

It was probably a dumb idea to push the issue, but why was he lying to her?

"What is it? If you give me the information, I can pick it up for you."

Busted. That was the look on Fernando's face. How was she supposed to learn to trust people when the first person she'd tried trusting was already lying to her? He didn't have the best track record, considering he'd already proven in their past that he wasn't trustworthy.

"I'd rather do it myself," he said. "But thanks."

Fernando stood back and gestured at the window opening he'd been working on. "As bad as this old barn looks, I don't think it will take as much work as you'd anticipated."

"That's great news," Shane said, joining them. "I'll

admit, I was leery of their plan to turn it into an event center, but I know it's been used for parties and things in the past. Helen used to talk about the dances her family had in here. It's not so much of a stretch to think we could use it for paid events."

Even though she was still annoyed at Fernando for lying to her about something so simple, she couldn't help smiling at Shane's description. She'd been so young when her father and Helen had divorced, she didn't remember Helen the way her sisters did. It seemed such a shame that she didn't have many memories of a woman who'd given them so much.

"Erin found more pictures in the attic," Nicole said, looking over at Shane. "She brought them over to Ricky's to see if Ricky could identify anyone in them. Once we get them back, we're going to make copies to hang in the event center when it's done, but we thought we'd see if the Colorado Historical Society would like them."

Shane didn't look surprised by the information, so Leah must have already told him. "Helen would have been pleased. She used to talk about going through all the old stuff in the attic to see if anything had historical value to the various historical societies in the state. Both her family and Ricky's were among the first to ranch this area."

Even though Helen had only been her former stepmother, Nicole felt a sense of pride at being connected to such a long-standing tradition.

"I would love to see the pictures," Fernando said. "And anything else you have that would give me a sense of what you're hoping to accomplish. Plus, I love history, so I'd be very interested to see what this old place looked like before."

Maybe she was being bratty again, and going back to grudge mode, but it was annoying to see how readily Shane had launched into a conversation with Fernando like he was part of their project. She'd just barely thought that maybe she could trust him, but now that she'd caught him in a lie, it only proved he hadn't really changed. And frankly, she didn't want to engage any more than she had to with him.

Fernando might have the necessary skill to train her horse and help with repairs around the ranch, but he'd just very clearly shown that any hope of friendship was totally out of the question.

This was why she wasn't willing to put herself out there and make new friends or give up her single status. Trust in the Lord, fine. But humans other than her family? Forget about it.

Fernando couldn't understand Nicole's sudden coldness toward him. She'd been blowing hot and cold, but after their discussion the other day about faith, he'd thought they were finally at a place of understanding, if not friendship.

He'd seen how she'd looked for him in the church. She'd probably been expecting him to sit with them. But how could he explain what a big deal it had been for him to go to church at all? He hadn't wanted to sit with them, then be introduced to their friends and expected to join in, where someone would invariably ask him about his past. He'd end up having to be evasive, which would make him seem shady, and everything would be uncomfortable. It would be worse if he were forced to confess about his past.

Been there, done that, and it had never been successful. Besides, he wasn't planning on staying around Columbine Springs for long, so it didn't seem wise to get to know anyone or try to make friends.

As Shane talked about the history of the ranch, Fernando could feel Nicole's glare intensify.

What had he done wrong?

The boys came running out of the house.

"Mr. Shane! Mom's ready for us to go to your house," Dylan said, sounding excited. "She says I was good, so I get to have another riding lesson today."

Ryan ran over to Shane and gave him a bear hug around the legs. "Me, too," he said.

Even though it wasn't an unusual sight, seeing Shane with the boys brought a pang to Fernando's heart. He'd felt the same way in church, watching all the families interacting with the close friends they'd made there. He might say he was happy enough with his life, but the truth was, it was lonely.

He hadn't wanted to walk past the fellowship table, brimming with cookies and coffee. Nor had he wanted to slip in and out unnoticed, carefully avoiding the couple waiting to pass out gift bags to new attendees.

But it was easier this way. Because when they found out about his past, none of them would be so eager to see him again. Truth be told, this stopover in Columbine Springs had been a relief for his uncle. His aunt had been afraid to have him hanging around with nothing to do for a month, because people might think Fernando was up to no good.

Shane pulled his cowboy hat off his head and put it on Ryan. "Here you go, cowboy."

"Hey!" Dylan said, putting his hands on his hips. "It's my turn to wear the hat."

He could tell Shane was trying to remember if he'd forgotten whose turn it was or if Dylan was just being difficult. Fernando took off his own hat.

"Want to wear mine for a while?"

Dylan ran to him, grinning. "Thanks!"

As Dylan strutted around proudly, Ryan started to pout. "I want to wear Mr. Nando's hat!"

"You have my hat," Shane told him.

"It's Fer-Nando, not Nando," Dylan said. "How can you wear his hat if you can't even say his name?"

The tiny argument caught Fernando off guard with a momentary wave of grief. Adriana used to call him Nando when she was being affectionate. It was strange how these tiny reminders brought pangs to his heart.

"It's okay," Fernando told them. "Nando is a nickname for Fernando. My sister used to—"

He shouldn't have looked over at Nicole as he spoke. Even with the space separating them, the sadness in her eyes was obvious. He'd thought they'd come to a good place with Adriana and his grief, but obviously, his memory of his nickname brought up something else for Nicole.

Leah had come upon them and touched his arm gently. "It's okay. I'm sure it's hard, speaking of your loss. I can help Ryan learn to say your name correctly."

"Don't," Fernando said. "I don't mind. I'm more worried about what set Nicole off this time. I thought we'd finally reached an understanding."

Nicole had retreated into the horse barn, and Leah followed his gaze. "Give her space," she said. "Just because she's finally okay with you doesn't mean that she's come to terms with her anger at Adriana."

Though he nodded, he couldn't help feeling like there was something more going on. "Do you think she's offended I didn't sit with you in church?"

"Maybe," Leah said. "I know she spent a lot of time looking for you."

He hadn't realized what a big deal going to church with them had been for Nicole. "Thanks," he said. "I didn't realize she'd wanted me to sit with you all, and we should have clarified what going to church with your family looked like."

Leah shrugged. "We're pretty casual. It's fine if you don't want to sit with us. I'm sure she was just anxious to try and make you feel welcome in our church."

The boys ran past them, waving their hats in the air and making horse noises.

"We should probably get going. I promised them riding time at Shane's. Don't worry about Nicole. She needs to process whatever is going on in her head, and then she'll be fine."

"All right," Fernando said. "You all have fun. I'm going to finish work on this window."

He turned back to what he'd been working on, pulling his small notebook out of his pocket. He was sure he'd had the right measurements with him when he'd gone into town this morning, but when he'd gotten into his truck after church and taken a moment to look at his list, he couldn't find it.

A wasted trip to town. And even more wasted time

remeasuring everything. He only had a month here, and he wanted to make the best use of his time.

He glanced over at the horse barn. Should he go try to see what he'd done to upset Nicole? Or should he take Leah's advice and give her space?

At this point, he was already behind where he'd hoped to get with the work today. Though some people thought it was wrong to work on Sundays because of keeping the Sabbath, for Fernando, the work was the only thing that kept him sane. He'd redo his measurements, finish the prep work he had planned for this area, then go clear his head with Snookie.

Some people said that horses often had the same personality as their owner. In Snookie's case, he was starting to wonder if maybe that was true. Nicole was a wounded woman, and it was obvious that Snookie had been hurt, too.

Could he find a way to help them both?

Foolishness. He had no business getting involved with Nicole. But it didn't hurt to pray and ask God to give Nicole what she needed for her healing. In the meantime, he'd do what he could to help the horse who meant so much to her and fix up the barn that the family was counting on for their future. Practical things like that, he could do. The rest, he'd leave up to the Lord.

Chapter Six

The next day, Nicole arrived home from work to find a commotion in her yard. Dylan and Ryan were sobbing in Leah's arms, and Shane and Fernando appeared to be exchanging angry words.

She jumped out of her car and ran toward them.

"What's going on?" she asked.

Shane turned to her, anger written all over his face. "I told you not to get that horse. I know we said Fernando could train her, but I'm done being patient. That horse is a danger. She went after the boys again. She bit Dylan."

Nicole's stomach hurt. That wasn't what she wanted at all.

Obviously she'd been selfish in thinking that a horse who needed love was more important than safety.

"Wait just a minute," Fernando said. "I've only been working with her a few days. You can't expect results overnight. You know that. I know you're worried about the boys, and I am, too. What were they doing in the barn in the first place?"

She looked over at Leah, who was holding Dylan in her arms. The boys might not have been allowed in the barn, but Snookie still bit him.

"I guess you have a point," Shane said grudgingly. "I don't rightly know what happened, but surely you can understand my concern seeing Dylan injured."

Fernando nodded. "I do. I'm concerned as well. What I'm also concerned with is what behavior was being exhibited around Snookie when she bit him. What was going on to make her want to bite? These factors all make a difference when it comes to knowing what to do. You can get rid of the horse, but that horse is just going to bite someone else."

Nicole's stomach clenched. Yes, she was concerned about her nephews' safety, but that didn't mean she wanted anyone else to be in danger.

Fernando turned to her. "I think we need to do more investigation. It's not natural for horses to bite for no reason, and I'd like the chance to find out why."

Even though this was about a horse, once again Nicole couldn't help thinking of the situation with Fernando. She'd yelled and accused, but until the other night, she'd never asked for Fernando's side of the story. She'd assumed it was cut-and-dried that Fernando was obviously not a very good person. Shame on her.

And even though she still felt guilty that Snookie had bitten her nephew, she couldn't help but feel a small amount of compassion for the horse. Fernando was right. From what she read, horses bit people for a variety of reasons, not all of which were the horse's fault.

She walked over to where her sister sat on the porch and smiled at Dylan. "What happened, buddy?"

Dylan sniffled. "Your mean horse bit me."

Nicole nodded and held her arms out to him. "I'm sure that was very scary."

Dylan nodded as he came to her, and as she wrapped her arms around him, his tears wet her shirt. How did you balance wanting to care for a horse, but also keeping a seven-year-old safe?

"How did it happen?" she asked him, ruffling his hair.

Dylan wiped his nose with the back of his sleeve as he pulled away. "Ryan threw my ball into the barn. I ran in to get it, and your horse was making all kinds of noises, like she was upset."

He looked thoughtful for a minute before continuing. "You were really late coming home from work, so I thought she was hungry and needed to eat. I grabbed some hay, and I held it out to her. Then she bit me in the arm."

The men had been slowly making their way toward them, and they were hovering nearby as Dylan made his proclamation. Both men looked thoughtful and nodded as they seemed like they were coming to the same conclusion as Nicole.

She turned to them. "So Dylan got bit because he was inappropriately feeding my horse."

Shane made a noise. "I guess so," he said. "But you've got to understand, if Snookie's behavior doesn't get under control, you're going to have to get rid of her. Dylan was in the wrong for going into the barn and then trying to feed her. However, that could've been anyone. You and I both know that Snookie likes to bite. I'm going to put it to you plain and clear. If Snookie bites one more person, she has to go."

Shane turned his attention to Leah. "I'll talk to the boys again and reemphasize our safety rules around horses. But, Nicole, you've got to do your part, too."

As Shane and the boys went inside, there was a part of Nicole that felt good to know how loving and protective Shane was of the boys. After everything they'd been through in their short lives, they deserved to have a man who cared so deeply for them.

But as Nicole walked toward the barn the pain in her heart and tightness in her chest made it almost too difficult to breathe. Could they get Snookie to stop biting?

Fernando stepped in next to her. "It's going to be okay," he said. "I know it seems hopeless, but Snookie isn't the first biter I've trained."

She sighed as she glanced up at him. "Yes, but you've said that change won't happen overnight. What if she bites someone else in the meantime?"

It still bothered her that he'd lied to her about having errands to run after church. Yes, it had been a white lie, but a lie was a lie, and after all the white lies he'd told to cover up his sister's affair with Brandon, Nicole couldn't help wondering how she could trust Fernando.

Were his reassurances about Snookie just more white lies designed to make Nicole feel better?

Fernando leaned on the rail and gestured at the horse. "We'll do everything we can to keep others out of the way and out of danger. I think Shane is being unfair, considering Dylan was at fault. Any horse will bite if you offer them food incorrectly."

While Nicole knew that to be true, she also knew the stubborn set to Shane's jaw.

"How do I know you're not just saying this to make me feel better?" Nicole asked.

Maybe she wasn't brave enough to directly call him out on his lies, but she needed him to know that she wasn't going to let him play the same smoke-and-mirrors game he'd been part of before.

He gave her a determined look, like she'd somehow offended his pride in asking the question. "Because I know horses. And I also would never put anyone in danger by overpromising results. It's dangerous for both horse and human."

In this, she believed him. Fernando's sins were about trying to protect people, or at least that seemed to be the thought process behind them. But he would never deliberately hurt someone.

So how did she make him understand that for her, being lied to was a deliberate wound?

Nicole shook her head. It wasn't like her relationship with Fernando was going anywhere. She didn't want, or need, for him to understand her emotions.

She looked over at Snookie, wanting to trust Fernando, but not sure if she could.

Fernando reached out and touched her arm gently. "It will be all right. Shane is just being a protective father."

Nicole nodded, but when she looked over and watched Shane with Leah and the boys, she could see the love between them and couldn't see Shane budging.

She turned back to Fernando. "Are you sure I wouldn't just be better off giving her away?"

That would solve a lot of problems.

But she loved Snookie. And sometimes she thought Snookie loved her. What was she supposed to do?

Nicole had gotten herself into this mess by not trusting in the Lord. She closed her eyes and sent a quick prayer heavenward that God would help her make the right choices when it came to her horse.

She didn't want to give up Snookie. But she also didn't want anyone else to get hurt.

"That's up to you," Fernando said. "I can tell you love Snookie and want to help her. I also know how much you love your family. If you're asking me if I think there is any danger, the answer is no. But I do think it's going to take some time to get her to a place where she is safe for everyone. I guess what you have to decide is whether or not you're willing to do the work."

Even though Nicole had a smile on her face, Fernando could see the questions in her eyes. He'd only been here a few days, and he hadn't had enough time to work with Snookie in a way that would give them any improvement. Shane was being harsh, too harsh, but Fernando understood.

The boys might not be his sons, but he loved them like any father would. That's how Fernando would feel if he had sons. No, he wasn't going to think about that. It wasn't possible for him, but if he were fortunate enough to have a family of his own, he would also probably be protective of his children. Then again, he knew how much being sheltered had hurt him growing up.

His mother had been so overprotective, afraid of him doing anything where he might get hurt. She'd sheltered both him and Adriana, and they had both rebelled. Fernando got mixed up with the wrong kind of crowd, and even though he could have gotten into worse trouble and had worse friends, he'd done enough damage to his life.

How did a parent balance keeping a child safe without holding on too tight?

None of this was useful to think about, not when he already knew it was impossible for him. But just because his dreams were out of reach didn't mean he couldn't help Nicole with hers.

"Is it worth it?" Nicole asked. "Am I kidding myself in thinking that we can get Snookie to behave?"

Fernando heard the sadness in her voice. The desire to keep her horse, but the fear that the work they did wouldn't be enough.

"I'm going to give your horse everything I have," he said. "The question is, will you?"

The fear in her eyes nearly broke his heart. He knew what it meant. She was already dealing with a broken heart. She'd been punishing him all these months because of it. This wasn't just a promise about a horse. It was a promise that Nicole's heart wouldn't be broken again.

Could he keep his promise? He sent a quick silent prayer that God would give him what he needed to be able to do so.

Nicole looked over at Snookie.

"I'm all she has," Nicole said. "No one else wanted her. I didn't tell Shane this part, but when I was looking at Snookie, I overheard some of the ranch hands talking about her only being good for dog food. They were going to send her to slaughter."

Monsters. It wasn't unheard of for a bad trainer to give up on a horse, but to send it to a slaughterhouse?

Though he'd heard of the practice, it seemed almost criminal.

How could he fault Nicole for wanting to save this horse?

The heartache in her voice as she spoke about Snookie being unwanted gave him a deeper glimpse into Nicole's heart. It had been broken because the man who promised to love her wanted someone else. How unloved must that have made Nicole feel? True, she had two wonderful sisters and two nephews who adored her. But the romantic connection was a special kind of love, a special kind of being wanted.

He couldn't be the man to heal Nicole's broken heart, but the horses in prison had healed his. Saving Snookie just might give Nicole the safe place to love and be loved. No, it wasn't romantic, but it was different from the love of a friend or family. It was a forever commitment between a deeply bonded horse and human, almost like a marriage.

"I promise you, no matter what happens, Snookie won't be sent to slaughter."

She gave a swift jerk of her head in affirmation, then they silently walked to Snookie, and he put a halter and rope on her.

Once Fernando brought Snookie to the round pen, he looked over at Nicole. "I want to start at the basics. I'm sure you've done all of this, but let's go back to the beginning. It's time for the two of you to bond."

She hesitated, and he gave her a smile. "I know it's scary, thinking you might have to let her go. But consider this. If you do have to give her up, you'll be sending a better horse to a new home. Maybe they can give her what she needs. You're at least preparing her for her future, regardless of what that future is."

Nicole nodded slowly. "I hadn't thought of it that way. It's like the kids I teach. At the end of the day, or at the end of the school year, I have to send them back to their parents. Even though some of them I love like my own and dearly wish I didn't have to let go. But all I can do is give them the tools they need to live a good life and be happy. I can do that for Snookie."

She squared her shoulders in a new way, looking stronger and more confident than she had a few minutes earlier. Connecting her work with the horse to her work with kids seemed to have given her the strength she needed.

He began basic gentling exercises with Snookie, taking her through what should be familiar motions, pleased that she responded well to his handling. He lunged her, watching for signs that Snookie was allowing him to lead her.

As the horse relaxed, he turned to Nicole. "It's your turn. I want you to use your body the way I have been and get her to join up with you."

He demonstrated the motion again and was pleased to see how Nicole quickly picked up on what he was asking her to do. One of the trainers he'd worked with had once told him that a horse could only be trained to the level of its trainer. Nicole and Snookie would do well together.

Once again, he thought back to how both horse and human had issues trusting. If they could learn to trust each other, it would be easier for them to trust others.

Even though Fernando had told Nicole that she would

be sending a better Snookie to someone who could handle her if she had to give her up, he knew it would be hard. It had nearly broken Fernando to have to give up the first horse he'd trained while in prison, but getting the second horse had taught him that it was okay to put your heart into an animal and let it go. And now he understood that love was about allowing yourself to participate in all the stages of caring, from creating that initial bond to the goodbye. Maybe forever, and maybe for now.

Someday, Fernando would have a place and horses of his own, where he wouldn't have to have that conversation with himself with every horse. He'd be able to keep the special ones. At least for as long as God was willing to let him have them.

Nothing in life was guaranteed, but Fernando had to be grateful for all the moments God had granted him. Which was how he had to view this time with Nicole. She was a special lady, and were his circumstances different, he'd want to pursue something more. To be a greater part of healing her heart than just giving her the tools via her horse.

But it wasn't meant to be, and this had to be enough.

He returned his focus to Nicole and Snookie. Snookie responded well to Nicole's directions, giving her what she asked for when she asked for it without a fight. Were someone to look in on what they were doing, they would think that training Snookie was effortless. But Nicole only made it look that way because she was doing all the right things.

Fernando stepped closer to Nicole. "I'm tricking the horse into thinking we are the same. Now I want you to raise your right hand and send her in the other direction."

Nicole did as he asked, and once again, the horse readily complied. They continued the motions, and then, as he could see Snookie softening toward Nicole, Fernando spoke quietly. "Be still," he said. "I want you to walk forward slowly, and I want you to hold your hand out gently behind you. Just be still. Quiet."

In the stillness of the moment, he could hear Nicole's breathing become softer, more relaxed. They'd both been working hard, but as she stilled, Snookie approached. Typically, the horse would give the trainer a little nudge, a sign of accepting the trainer into its herd. Snookie came and rested her head right on Nicole's shoulder.

"She's joined up with you," Fernando said softly. "Let her know that you're here for her. That you accept her. Very slowly, give her a gentle touch."

As Nicole reached up and touched Snookie's nose, Fernando could feel the tears hitting the backs of his eyes. The bond between human and horse was apparent, and he could see the love between them. Maybe Snookie didn't know it was love, but she was giving Nicole her trust. And that, for a horse, was about the closest thing one could get to love.

Maybe that's why relationships with horses were so much easier. They didn't care about your past, what you'd done, or anything other than how you treated them in that moment. True, if you'd ever hurt a horse, especially a mustang, it wasn't something forgotten, but as long as you gave them that same tender love, that was something they would also never forget.

Nicole needed this kind of love. Fernando couldn't pretend he understood what it was like to be betrayed by your best friend and fiancé, and to fully know what was behind the pain in her eyes whenever the past came up, but he did know betrayal. And he understood what it felt like to lose everything you thought you had worth living for.

The radical acceptance of the horse could give Nicole the strength to face her pain and move forward with her life. It was the closest Fernando could get to sharing his feelings for her.

Though Fernando wasn't living the life he'd hoped for himself, he hadn't come out of prison with the same feeling of worthlessness a lot of men had. He knew the love of God, the love of horses and, deep down, a love of himself. The only difference was, society didn't seem to love him back. Or at least they weren't willing to see past his label to the man he'd become.

Nicole, though, could draw on the strength she was gaining here and use it to propel her dreams to wherever she wanted them to take her.

As he walked along the side of the horse, focusing his attention on the back side of Snookie, Nicole caught his eye. "I've done this before with her, but it seems different. Maybe because we didn't quite do the join up the way you did. But I sense a change in her. And I feel like our bond is stronger."

He nodded. "That's the idea. Sometimes we rush the bond, or we think we have it, so we move on to the next step. But I want us to spend the next few days just doing this with her. Just bonding and letting her know she is safe."

That was the trouble with a lot of people, and with

life. They rushed what they wanted and pushed too hard, too soon, ending up with a shell of what they'd hoped for.

In a way, Fernando realized, that's what he had done in trying to get Nicole to forgive him. He had pushed too hard and tried too hard to get her to understand his way of thinking. He should have been more gentle and patient with her, rather than demanding. He should have remembered the lessons he'd learned in horse training.

"How will this stop her from biting?" Nicole asked, looking up from Snookie.

He felt the horse tense as he ran a hand along the ridge on her back. A scar. Probably from being whipped too hard. "Horses bite for a lot of reasons. She's exploring, but she also knows it's a good way to protect herself. We just have to show her that she doesn't need to protect herself anymore. And, like with children, we have to teach her when it's not okay to put things in her mouth."

As Nicole nodded once again, he saw more confidence in her eyes. She seemed more open and less afraid. Like the lessons that were healing Snookie were working in Nicole's heart as well.

Nicole's love for Snookie was so deep and real that even though she was preparing herself to potentially let the horse go, he didn't know that he could watch her do it.

Maybe Fernando and Nicole would never get to a place where things were good between them. But he would do everything in his power to make sure Nicole's heart didn't get broken again.

Chapter Seven

Even though Fernando wasn't standing inappropriately close to her, Nicole could sense his presence. Something about having him so near made her feel safe. Odd, considering she never thought she would feel safe in the same town as him because of all the bad feelings she had toward him.

His gently whispered instructions gave her confidence as she worked Snookie. And as he tweaked her motions ever so slightly, she could understand why the things she had been doing weren't working. Subtle differences, but enough for her to see that she had been going about it all wrong. It was comforting to know she had someone on her side.

Or at least partially. She still wasn't sure that she could trust him on a personal level, given his lie, but the change in her relationship with Snookie told her she could trust him with her horse.

Maybe that was enough. What she'd wanted in a horse was a companion to be there for her. A best friend. Someone she could tell her secrets to, who wouldn't run off with the man she loved or make her question everything about herself. Yes, she had her sisters, but this was different. And as much as she loved them, there was a hole in her heart they couldn't fill.

And then, just as she was beginning to think Fernando had almost become a part of her, he was gone. In his place was Snookie, standing behind her and following her lead.

Joining up with Snookie was almost as if Snookie was giving her a deeper level of love and trust. Respect. Like she was fully accepted into Snookie's herd. There was a deeper level of respect in the horse's demeanor toward her, but more than that, there was a sense of submission. The way Snookie was submitting to her, it was a sign that Nicole had earned it. Snookie wasn't giving her the signs out of fear, anger, frustration or any negative emotion. This was what Nicole had been hoping to accomplish.

As she connected with her horse in this moment, she knew she had Snookie's heart.

Maybe it was foolish of her to do so, since she hadn't seen it on a video or read it in a book, but she couldn't help putting her arms around the horse's neck and hugging her tight. "I love you, Snookie," she said.

Snookie responded by resting her head on Nicole's shoulder, gently, submissively, lovingly.

For a few moments she stood there, hugging her horse, feeling the love between the two of them. Then Fernando's voice behind her brought her back to reality.

"You've done good," he said. "I think we're at a good point now, because the last thing Snookie will remember leaving this arena is that she can trust you. Tomorrow, we'll work more with her, but for now, I think she needs a break."

Nicole released her hold on Snookie and then she turned and hugged Fernando. "Thank you," she said. "What just happened here, it's something I've dreamed of my whole life. I always wanted this kind of bond with a horse, and until now, I always thought it was out of my reach."

He returned her hug for a brief second, then pulled away. She probably shouldn't have hugged him. Though she'd thought they'd shared a few moments of connection, her touch obviously made him uncomfortable. Sometimes only one person felt the spark, which she'd clearly found out with Brandon. What she'd thought was love had been some other emotion on his part.

Nicole didn't need anything weird between her and Fernando. Especially because he'd already proven to her that she couldn't trust him. It was better for both of them this way. Whatever these emotional moments she felt were, she had to keep them to herself.

"Thank you. I'm just doing my job," Fernando said.

"Until now, I wasn't sure I could believe it was possible that I could keep Snookie. But now, I can see it."

He nodded slowly. "We're not out of the woods yet. We haven't done anything to address her biting, but now that you've bonded with her, it will be easier to break the habit. We still have a long way to go, but I believe we can get there."

As they walked Snookie back to the barn, Nicole's heart felt lighter and happier than it had in a long time. And yet, she felt a surprising weariness as well. They tied Snookie up, and Fernando handed her a brush.

"She doesn't need a very thorough brushing, but we should keep reinforcing the idea that normal horse care is good for her and we aren't going to hurt her."

She started brushing Snookie and noticed that Fernando was doing the same on the other side, speaking softly so she couldn't hear what he was saying.

"I'm sorry, I didn't catch that," she said.

He looked up at her. "I wasn't talking to you. Sorry. I was talking to God. Praying for Snookie."

They'd had a conversation about his spiritual connection to the animals before, but she hadn't observed just how deep it was.

But in the sincere expression on Fernando's face, she saw an earnest connection to God that made her curious. Especially since things had been so weird with him going to church.

"Do you think it helps?"

Fernando gave a shrug. "It can't hurt. Besides, I think animals, as God's creatures, have a deeper connection to God, only we don't understand it. So why not talk to God and see where God leads me with these animals?"

Nicole tried to understand his perspective as she continued brushing Snookie. "I just don't know what to believe about God anymore," she said. "How do we know what is God and what is just wishful thinking on our part?"

Weird, that she would admit this to Fernando when it wasn't something she'd expressed to anyone else. In her small group at church, full of women who seemed to be so happy all the time, without the same crushing disappointments she'd faced in her life, it seemed wrong to share her doubts. And yet, saying so in front of Fernando, who already knew most of her dark secrets, didn't seem so threatening.

Which made everything even more confusing for her. She had no proof she couldn't trust the women from church, but she couldn't open up to them. And yet she had evidence that Fernando wasn't to be trusted, yet she confessed all this weird stuff to him.

Fernando set his brush down, then came around the other side of the horse. "Maybe we don't. But maybe that's the point of having faith. Of believing that we have a good God who loves us and trusting that even when we don't understand something, it will work out for the best."

He ran his fingers along the scarred section of Snookie's back. "When I first met her, she would freak out if I touched her here. This was a place where someone had hurt her. But somehow, she's gotten over it. Is it because I prayed? Is it because I have some kind of special touch? I don't know. But every day, I touch her here, and I ask God to heal her hidden wounds. When I work with her, I ask God to give me what I need. Maybe God hasn't answered those prayers. Maybe it's just a trick of my imagination. But when I work with Snookie, I always have what I need and know exactly what to do. Just as important, I have seen the way she no longer flinches at my touch."

He moved his hands to another set of scars. "So I don't know. Maybe it isn't God. But the whole point of faith is choosing to believe. Believe that God is working here, and maybe He is or maybe He isn't. But I find it easier to know and trust that God is with me."

No one had ever spoken to her with such a deep belief in trusting God. Well, they had, but she'd never seen it so deep in another human. Sure, they talked about it in church, but it always seemed more on a theoretical level, since she never saw this type of faith in them. Then again, how could she, when she hadn't really taken the time to get to know them? She'd been too busy pretending everything was okay and shutting everyone out. Maybe the women she thought had no problems were just like her. Full of pain, but too scared to let anyone in.

Could she give them a chance?

Fernando pointed at a brush on a nearby bench. "Can you hand me that brush? There's something stuck in Snookie's mane, and I'd like to see if I can get it out."

It took a moment to register what he was asking, so when she turned to get the brush, Fernando was already on his way. She ran into him, and when she did, it wasn't the oops feeling of having made a mistake, but a sensation of—

What on earth was that?

No.

The unexpected electric jolt she felt running into his rock-hard chest was just a silly reaction. Why she kept having it, she didn't know, but it was getting to be crazy.

"Sorry," Fernando muttered, stepping away.

She thought she spied a tinge of red on his cheeks as he turned his back to her. Had she embarrassed him? Then she looked down at her hand and realized it had been on his chest far too long, and she probably made him uncomfortable.

She was making herself uncomfortable, dwelling on that weird moment, so it was no wonder.

Hadn't she just given herself a talking-to about not

putting Fernando in awkward positions? And that she couldn't trust him on a personal level?

That was the trouble with trying to keep things strictly business when they had so much personal baggage between them. And, as much as she hated to admit it, if it weren't for their past, she'd find him attractive.

She willed herself to stop going down that path. Fernando wasn't the man for her.

"No," she said. "I'm sorry. My mind was elsewhere, and I wasn't thinking."

He grabbed the brush he'd asked her for and headed back to the horse. "Don't worry about it. You look a little flushed. You've probably had too much sun. Let me just get this knot out and you can put Snookie out to pasture, and I'll get us both some water."

Nicole took a deep breath and tried to stop noticing how aware she was of Fernando as a man.

Sure, she'd joked with Adriana about having a hottie brother before, but this was different. Now she saw him as a man, with the compassion to help an emotionally wounded woman who hated him and a horse no one else wanted, who was deeply connected to the Lord. The fact that Fernando was one of the most handsome men she'd ever met was only icing on the cake.

"I don't hate you anymore," Nicole blurted.

"I know." Fernando held up the brush and smiled at her. "But don't mistake the gratitude you're feeling for anything else."

Could she be any more mortified? He'd obviously noticed the weird spark she'd felt and was trying to gently tell her that he didn't return her feelings. Awkward!

Worse, she already knew that he was bad for her.

Why was she attracted to a man who was obviously the worst possible choice for her?

"I'm not," she reassured him. "I'm just…reevaluating."

She took another deep breath. Fernando seemed to pray about everything. Maybe it wouldn't hurt to pray about whatever this was between them.

Fernando had told her that he relied on God's strength, and while she definitely agreed with the principle, she didn't know how she was supposed to do that. Or what praying in this situation would accomplish.

But since Brandon's death, she'd lost the wide-eyed trust she'd had, and the only people she could count on for having her back were her sisters. Mostly, though, she relied on herself.

Admitting that she had been relying on herself too much also meant admitting that she honestly had no idea what to do anymore. Fernando had clearly come into her life for a reason, and even though it had caused her so much pain in the beginning, she could see where it was also bringing her healing. God had brought the man she hated the most in the world to her to help her.

So what were these weird feelings between her and Fernando?

Fernando finished brushing out the knot, untied Snookie and handed her the rope.

She might not be able to sort out whatever was going on with her and Fernando, but she could take care of her horse.

"Good girl," Nicole said, patting Snookie. Snookie gave her a little nudge, like she was saying that she knew.

As she returned to the barn after putting Snookie

in the pasture, Fernando came out carrying a bottle of water but giving her a wide berth.

It had been awkward for him, too. He probably thought that once again, he'd unintentionally hurt her. But it seemed weird to reassure him, to make more of what it had seemingly been.

"I got you some water," he said. "Sometimes we get so caught up in working that we forget to drink, and it's important to stay hydrated out here."

She smiled at him and took the bottle. "Thanks. Sorry about earlier. I should have been looking where I was going."

He shook his head. "No, it was my fault. I should've been, too."

She laughed. "We're not going to play a game of who is more at fault, are we? No harm was done, so let's call it even."

Maybe that would be enough to get the moment out of her mind.

He stared at her briefly, and in his gaze, she could see that he had felt something, too.

Maybe the whole point of this was to remind her that she needed to rely on God's strength for the answer.

Okay, then. Nicole took a deep breath.

God, I don't know what this is all about. But I'm willing to open myself up to whatever possibility You're leading me to as long as You can give me the strength to get through it.

Fernando tried acting nonchalant as he drank his water. That moment with Nicole…wow! Could she see that his hand was shaking?

It seemed unjust that as much as he'd harbored a wish to someday find a woman who could love him, he would now have this feeling with Nicole. Fine, he'd had a secret crush on her off and on over the years, but this was different. Nicole's hand on his chest, while only the briefest of touches, had something almost electric in it. An exchange of energy that brought a light into her eyes that hadn't been there before.

Part of him wanted to take her into his arms, kiss her and see if they could turn these feelings into something that would last. But the more practical side of him knew that she only knew the good part of the man, the part that wouldn't ruin her life.

He could feel her watching him as they drank their water in silence. If he told her the truth about his past, it would end things right now. But as he tried to form the words that would be the nail in the coffin for anything that might be, he found he couldn't.

It wasn't just about the spark he'd felt when she'd touched him. But it seemed like some of the sadness had lifted off her. Could he break her heart so quickly? Or was he imagining all of this?

Crazy. All this nonsense from one innocent touch.

He'd leave it alone for now. No good could come of acknowledging his feelings for her, or of seeing if she had feelings for him. His only job was to guide her in training her horse. And God help him, that's all it was going to be about. He offered another prayer that God would give him strength to do what needed to be done, drained the rest of his water bottle and tossed it into the recycle bin.

And even though he knew he probably shouldn't, he

couldn't help stealing another peek at Nicole as he put away the rest of the brushes and tack. Which led him to issuing one more plea to God that they wouldn't get their hearts broken. An inevitable outcome if Nicole was developing any sort of feelings for him and she discovered the truth about his past.

Time for some good old-fashioned manual labor. He'd gone into town earlier for the parts he'd wanted, but they'd had to order them, so he was going to tackle clearing out more of the interior of the barn. It had been used for storage for years, according to Shane, and even though they'd gotten all the important items out, there was still a large number of things to deal with.

The interior of the barn looked like it had once housed animals, then when the horse barn had been built, this one had been converted to hay and equipment storage and then just storage. The ranch must have been successful at one point in time. Maybe it could be restored to its former glory.

As Fernando passed some falling-down walls that had probably been stalls, he could see the family's vision for turning this into an event center. He wouldn't be able to do all the work, but he could put together a good enough foundation that whoever they brought in for cleanup and finish would have an easier time of things.

The main hay storage area would make for a great large event room. Based on plans Erin had shown him, they were going to put an industrial kitchen on one end and restrooms along the east wall, and the upper level would be a cozy seating area or space for smaller events.

Which meant all these old stalls along the west side

needed to go. Even if they were meant to be rooms, they would still need to be torn down and reframed.

Fernando picked up the crowbar he'd left lying there the last time he'd worked on this section. As he pried loose some of the boards, it felt good to be able to take his frustrations out on something he could easily fix. The thing he'd always loved about construction was that during all stages of the project, he could see his progress and where everything stood.

With the horse, and Nicole, nothing was as easy to determine. Their relationship seemed to have a weird up and down progression, and just when he thought they were on an even keel, things got messed up again. In some ways, it wasn't so different from earning trust from a horse. And that, he knew, was all about patience. Being consistent and loving through all the ups and downs, and...

Loving?

Fernando pried another board loose. The idea of loving Nicole seemed easy enough in the theoretical sense, like you'd love a horse, or a fellow human being in the name of God. But the feelings he had for Nicole tended to move him into different, more troubling waters.

And that's where he had no idea what he was doing. *Please, God, help me.*

It was the only prayer he knew how to pray when he wasn't even sure what he was praying for. What did Nicole need? What did Fernando need? And how was Fernando supposed to act accordingly?

Not having a wife and family to love hadn't bothered him so much until now. But as he heard Leah's boys playing somewhere in the distance, the ache in

Fernando's heart was almost too much to bear. He'd be lying if he said Nicole hadn't stirred something in him, something he'd thought had been dead a long time.

The scariest thing about the moment of attraction he'd shared with Nicole was that he hadn't experienced it in so long that it was harder to dismiss than he'd thought. Even now, the image of the look in her eyes was crisp in his memory.

There was something between them, but they both had more reason to run from it than to pursue it.

So what was Fernando supposed to do, given the impossibility of the situation?

Lord, please help me.

Chapter Eight

They'd been making progress with Snookie over the past week, and Nicole was pleased to see that not only had Snookie not bitten anyone, she hadn't even tried. However, they were careful to keep the boys far away from the horse.

And whatever weirdness had passed between Nicole and Fernando the previous week hadn't happened again, even though they'd been in close quarters, working with the horse.

Maybe it was a weird fluke, and, like Fernando had said, dehydration.

Which was why, Sunday after church, as she sat on the church steps, eating cookies with her nephews, it didn't bother her to see Fernando getting in his truck and driving off.

She'd seen him sneak out at the end of the service, but judging from the welcome bag in his hand, whoever had been on greeter duty had caught him before he could get far.

It was so weird that he seemed uncomfortable with church, given his deep love of the Lord.

But that was between Fernando and God. It had nothing to do with him training her horse or even working on their barn. She wasn't going to allow their relationship to become any more personal. That seemed to be where they always got in trouble.

"Hi, Nicole!" Janie came up to her, and her little boy, Sam, tugged at Dylan's arm.

"Come play football with us!"

Dylan looked at Nicole for permission, and Nicole nodded. The boys ran off, laughing, and Nicole smiled. It was nice to see everyone finding their place here in Columbine Springs.

Which left Nicole. He'd hidden Brandon and Adriana's affair from her, and even though Fernando had apologized and Nicole was working on forgiving him, he'd lied to her again.

She didn't think she could ever fully trust someone the way she had Brandon and Adriana, but maybe she could make some friends and at least have a few girlfriends to hang out with from time to time.

"I really liked what you said in Bible study today," Janie said, sitting next to Nicole. "About grief and how God gives us all our own ways of processing it, so we can't tell others how to do it. It sounds like you've lost someone close to you."

Nicole hadn't known why she'd volunteered that information. She usually didn't talk much in their Bible study group, not wanting to sound stupid or reveal too much about herself.

But as she saw the sincerity on Janie's face, she realized that maybe opening up wasn't so bad.

"Yes," Nicole said. "I did. And it's hard for me, having people tell me how I should feel or what I should do. It's more complicated than people make it seem."

Janie gave her a small smile. "I agree. It's hard to talk about grief because everyone has an opinion about it, and you're just trying to get through."

Maybe she had been wrong in not trying to make friends sooner.

A football landed at their feet.

"Mom, you were supposed to catch that," Sam shouted.

Janie picked the ball up and threw it back to the boys.

Then she turned back to Nicole, shaking her head. "I promised Sam I'd play with them after church. But I'd really love to chat with you some more. Any chance you're free for coffee…" Janie quickly glanced down at her phone, then back at Nicole. "Tomorrow? I have some time while Sam's at soccer, or we could try later in the week."

Nicole watched as the singles group gathered by their usual spot to discuss where to go to lunch afterward. She still wasn't ready to join them, but maybe she could start slow with Janie.

"Sure. I'd like that."

Even though the words came out sounding like a rote response, at Janie's smile, Nicole realized she meant it. As Janie got up, Nicole looked for her sisters, who were both busy chatting with other people from the church.

One of the little girls, Gracie, who was in Nicole's

preschool class, came up to her and handed her a picture. "I made this for you!"

It was of a man, a woman and a little girl. "Who are these people?"

"That's my daddy, that's you and that's me. My mommy died when I was little, and I need a mommy who lives here with me. You're my favorite teacher, so maybe you could be my mommy."

Nicole's heart broke a little at the sadness in Gracie's voice. She didn't even know what to say in response.

Fortunately, before she could answer, a harried-looking man approached. "Gracie! I told you not to run off."

Gracie turned to look at him. "Daddy, this is my teacher, Miss Nicole. She's the one I want to be my mommy."

An embarrassed look crossed the man's face. Nicole had never met Gracie's father because Gracie's grandmother did all the drop-offs and pickups at school.

"Hi." Nicole stood and held out her hand. "I'm Nicole Bell. So nice to finally meet you. Gracie talks about you a lot."

He looked like he was embarrassed, so Nicole gave him the warmest smile she could. "Don't worry about the mommy thing. I get it on a regular basis. If it's not one of the kids wanting me to be their mommy, it's one of them wanting to marry me. Preschoolers don't understand the subtleties of adulthood sometimes."

Gracie's dad nodded slowly. "Thanks. Everyone says it's just a phase." Then he smiled down at Gracie. "She never really knew her mother, and now that she's aware of all her friends having one, it's confusing to her that she doesn't. I'm Evan Duncan, by the way. She talks a lot about you, too, so I'm glad to finally meet you."

He was handsome, and she'd heard some of the ladies in the women's group talking about what a catch he was. But nothing about him stirred even the slightest bit of romantic curiosity. In fact, her mind strayed to Fernando, even though he was the last man she should have been thinking about.

Pushing those thoughts away, she turned her attention back to Evan. "I'm glad to meet you as well. Please let me know if there's anything I can do to make things easier for Gracie."

Then she smiled down at the little girl. "Other than becoming her mommy, that is."

Gracie gave a little pout, but Evan ruffled her hair. "Thanks for being so understanding. I'm hoping things with work will slow down soon so I can be around more."

As Evan left with Gracie, Nicole stared down at the picture the little girl had given her. She'd always hoped to have a family of her own someday. But how was she supposed to do that when she'd already shown such bad judgment in men? The first man she'd thought she was going to marry turned out to be a liar and a cheat, and she didn't seem to be attracted to seemingly nice guys like Evan. No, the only man who stirred anything in her was someone who'd already proven himself to not be trustworthy.

Maybe the real person Nicole couldn't trust was herself.

She thought about her conversations with Fernando, and how even the sermons at church lately had been about trusting in the Lord. Today's lesson had been about trusting in the Lord when things don't go your way, which was where the conversation about grief in their Bible study had come up.

Things certainly hadn't been going Nicole's way until they'd moved to Columbine Springs. And even then, it seemed like everything was a crazy journey of ups and downs.

What did it all mean?

She stared at her Bible and asked God once again to guide her as she tried navigating this new life. Life on the ranch made her happy, and she'd thought it the fulfillment of so many of her childhood dreams.

But it was also bringing challenges she hadn't counted on—like her dream horse being a much larger project than she'd ever imagined.

Erin came and sat beside her. "Bible study was pretty intense, wasn't it?"

"Yeah." Nicole smiled at her sister. "But Janie came over and talked to me a little, and I don't feel so weird about speaking up."

Erin put her arm around Nicole. "You should never feel weird about speaking up. I felt kind of bad, because I realized that with all three of us facing so many losses on top of one another, I didn't do such a good job of listening to you and what you needed."

Nicole leaned into Erin and rested her head on her shoulder. "You did the best you could, given your own grief at the time. I love you for that."

"Thanks. I kind of feel like a jerk for pushing you toward Fernando, saying that you two can help each other with your shared grief. Maybe that's not what you need."

Closing her eyes, Nicole tried to think about what she did need. The truth was, she wasn't sure anymore.

"It's okay," Nicole said, looking up at her sister. "The situation with Fernando is complicated, and I don't have a clue as to what to do with it."

Erin gave her another squeeze. "I'm trying to stay out of it, but for what it's worth, I don't think he's a bad guy. He seems to genuinely care about you. So maybe you should talk to him about whatever is complicating things for you and see where that goes. Sometimes I think most of our problems with others happen because we don't talk about what's going on and we let it fester for too long."

"But what if we don't know if we can trust the other person to tell the truth?"

That was the real issue. Should she talk to Fernando about the things on her mind? Should she clarify that weird moment of attraction so they were on the same page? Certainly. But how would she be able to trust in his answers?

"Good question," Erin said. "I don't have an easy answer for you, because it depends. But I think that's where you have to learn to trust. Sometimes, you'll be disappointed, but you learn from your mistakes, and other times, you're going to be pleasantly surprised."

Ryan ran up to them. "Mom says it's time to go."

Nicole straightened and realized the churchyard had thinned out. She'd told Fernando that she wanted to work with Snookie this afternoon, and here she was, keeping him from whatever else he had to do today.

When she got home, Snookie stood tied to the rail, wearing a saddle.

Nicole reached out and patted the horse, glad they seldom dressed up for church, so she could get right to work. "Good girl," she said. Snookie gave her a soft nudge, acknowledging her presence and making it seem like she was happy to see her.

Fernando came out from around the other side of the barn. "Oh, good. You're home. I was hoping to give you some saddle time today."

He untied Snookie and they led her into the round pen. She watched as he began the same basic exercises he always took Snookie through before a ride. Watching him work made her think about how it reflected on his character. She'd said she trusted Fernando with her horse, but not as a person. Animals were said to be good judges of character.

Could there be more to Fernando's lies than what she'd originally thought? Maybe to him, the white lies weren't a big deal, and he didn't know how damaging they were to their relationship.

Fernando paused as he took his hat off and wiped his brow. Though they hadn't been working long, Fernando had probably been out in the sun for a while, since he'd left church so much earlier than she had.

"Can I get you water or something?" Nicole asked when he directed his gaze toward her.

He nodded. "*Sí*. I'd like that."

His brief move to speaking Spanish confirmed her suspicion of how hard he'd been working. She'd noticed that he fell back on it when he was tired or frustrated.

When she returned to the round pen with his water,

Fernando walked over to her, leading the horse behind him. "Thank you," he said. "You didn't have to do that, but I'm glad you did. I can't believe how warm it's gotten out here."

"And it's only going to get warmer," Nicole said. "I understand we're due for some record highs later in the week."

He nodded slowly. "We have a few more days of cooler weather we can take advantage of."

Fernando drank the water. "Much better," he said. He reached for his hat, like he was going to take it off and pour some water on his head, but then seemed to realize that he couldn't hold the water bottle in one hand and the horse in the other and accomplish the task.

"Want me to hold Snookie for you?" she asked.

He nodded. "That would be great. If you want, you can do the exercise with her I just was."

She tried focusing on his words as he dumped water on his head and ran his fingers through his hair. Though she'd been praying for clarity about her relationship with Fernando, moments like these were only more distracting. It seemed crazy that she was finding him even better-looking.

Nicole took a deep breath and gave Snookie a pat. This had to be her focus. Not the handsome man giving her instructions.

As Nicole went through motions she'd watched Fernando do, she could see where patience was so important in working with horses. Fernando had been emphasizing patience in all his lessons, and maybe those lessons applied elsewhere in her life as well.

All the answers she was looking for just needed time and patience.

"Nice job," Fernando said.

The small praise made her heart do a tiny somersault. She did feel something for him, and spending the week denying it hadn't changed anything.

She shifted her weight, and Snookie did a weird side step, causing Nicole to lose her balance. Fernando was at her side quickly as she tumbled into his arms.

"I'm okay," she said. "I wasn't expecting that, that's all. But I'm fine now."

Was it her imagination, or was he holding her a little more tightly than one would do with a mere business associate? Even though he was hot and sweaty, he smelled good. Like leather, horse and something a little spicy.

She fought the temptation to stay in his arms a little longer to breathe in his scent but instead pulled away, then returned to her position in one of the stirrups.

Fernando nodded slowly. "I see that. I'm sorry if I was a little quick on my reaction. From my angle, it looked like you were in for a bad fall, and I didn't want you to get hurt. I don't want to give Shane any excuse for saying you can't work with Snookie anymore."

She hopped down from the stirrup and landed on the ground, facing him. "Has he said anything more to you?"

Fernando shook his head. "No, but I see how he watches us. How he looks at you. He and your sister may not be married yet, but I can tell that he already considers you his sister. I know how protective a man can be of his sister."

His voice caught, and she knew he was thinking

about Adriana. How had he been able to grieve her? From her friendship with Adriana, she knew that Fernando was a protective older brother, always looking out for her. It must be very difficult for him, knowing what happened to his sister and that he couldn't protect her or save her. Suddenly, Nicole felt very selfish for making the grief of the accident all about her.

"You miss Adriana, don't you?"

He nodded slowly, but she could see the questions on his face, like he wasn't sure he was supposed to answer her question that way.

"It's okay to miss her. She was your sister. If it were my sisters, I would miss them, too."

Something about giving Fernando permission to grieve Adriana unleashed something in her as well. Like she was letting go of her own pain, her own grudges, and she felt freer of her burdens than she had in a long time.

The thought of Adriana didn't hurt as much as it once did. She couldn't help expressing a silent prayer of gratitude for the healing God had brought into her life through Fernando. She never would have expected it, and, in fact, had fought it. And now she almost wished she hadn't. Maybe she would have found this peace a lot sooner.

"It's hard, knowing the right thing to do," he said. "I did my best to warn her off, and I've spent a lot of my life trying to protect her. And even though you know you don't have complete control over things, it's still hard to let go."

Even though she'd already apologized to him many times, she loosened her grip on the reins and stepped forward to give Fernando a gentle hug. "I'm so sorry for your loss. And I'm so sorry for how I treated you over it."

He hugged her back, and even though he had said he'd forgiven her many times and everything was good between them, this felt like they had reached a new place in their relationship. Like there was finally a mutual understanding of how complicated everything was, and that they were both willing to accept each other in the midst of all these messy details.

Snookie placed her head on Nicole's shoulder, giving her a little nudge. She loosened her hold on Fernando and gave the horse a pat. "Don't worry, Snookie. You'll always be my first love. My only love."

Fernando stepped back, chuckling. "She's definitely a jealous girl," he said. "In a way, that's good. It shows that she's bonded to you, and you mean a lot to her."

Then he gave Snookie a playful shove. "But you're not the boss of her. Nicole is the boss, and don't you forget it."

His eyes were laughing even though his voice was firm, and Nicole repeated the gesture. "That's right. I'm the boss."

She couldn't say it with as confident a tone as Fernando had, and that only made Fernando chuckle a little harder.

"You've got to say it like you mean it." He smiled at her again. "Think about the kids you teach. They're sweet and cute, and you just want to hug and cuddle them. But you've also got to give them a fair amount of discipline or else they'll walk all over you and turn into monsters."

Nicole laughed as she nodded. "And trust me, they do turn into monsters. All those cute little darlings, always getting their own way. They can be a nightmare."

"What made you want to work with children? With the way you love animals, I would think you would want to go to vet school or something."

Nicole shrugged. "We went to a career day when we were in school, and one of the places we got to visit was a vet. The first time they gave a horse a shot, I almost passed out. I knew I couldn't do that."

"It will save you a lot of money if you learn how to give your animal shots yourself. If we need to do anything with Snookie while I'm here, I'll be happy to show you. Otherwise, ask Shane about it. I'm sure he'll have no trouble helping you."

She knew that Fernando's time here was only temporary. And yet, hearing him talk about leaving made her feel bad. Who would've thought that now she wasn't sure the man she was so desperate to get rid of should actually leave?

"Have you thought about staying?" Nicole asked. "I'm sure some of the other ranchers could use a good trainer. Like I said, the guy I almost went with was super expensive, and the waiting list to get on with him was so long. Having another trainer around here would be amazing. Not only would the ranchers have more options, but I think you're much better with horses than the other guy was."

He gave her a weird look. "My uncle is expecting me."

"But you said he had no problem with you staying here to train a horse. He obviously doesn't need you that badly. And from what Adriana used to say about him, he isn't that great of a guy. Why would you go to a job you don't love when you can be training horses?"

Fernando supposed it was an innocent question, but Nicole had no idea how much it actually stung. He'd give just about anything to be a horse trainer. And the thought of staying here, in Columbine Springs, was more tempting than she could ever know. He loved this tiny little town, and even though he'd only gone to church twice, he loved the little church. The people here were so nice, so genuine, and he liked the way the community seemed to be a real community. He tried not to laugh as he remembered Bob and Jan Adams racing out with a gift bag to welcome him today. He hadn't wanted to get to know anyone or establish ties, but it seemed like they were intent on having it be otherwise.

The gift bag was filled with tiny, thoughtful treasures— a mug with the church's logo that said, "As much as coffee sustains you, trust in the Lord will sustain you more"; a handy pamphlet featuring Bible studies to get involved with, volunteer opportunities and contact information for the church; a Bible; a notebook; a pen; some candy; and a couple of homemade cookies he suspected came from the refreshment table he'd been afraid to pass by.

All things designed to anchor him in their church.

Jan had even hugged him when he left, telling him that she was happy to have him there.

But would they still accept him when they knew who he really was and what he had done?

"It's a good job," he said, trying to expel any thoughts of staying from his head. "Horse training is feast or famine. Even though you say I would have plenty of clients, how can you be so sure? This other guy might be known to the ranchers, so they might be more comfortable with him. It's better for me to take the job with my uncle, where I'm certain I will have constant work as opposed to going out on my own and not knowing."

Nicole gave him a funny look. "But you don't know that. At least ask Shane to introduce you to some of the other ranchers. I just heard him talking the other day about one of his friends who was having a hard time with one of his horses. Maybe he could introduce you to that guy. And maybe, if the guy likes you—"

"Stop right there. That's an awful lot of maybes. I can't rest my future on that. The only reason I can be here is because I had a month before the job with my uncle starts. But then I need to go and do the right thing."

Nicole shook her head. "But how is the right thing you going to work for your uncle? You can't say you love construction. I see the happiness on your face when you're working with Snookie. But when you're working on the buildings around the farm, doing construction stuff? You don't look like you hate it, but it's certainly not the same happiness you exude when you're with horses."

Why couldn't she let this go? What business of hers was it, anyway?

"I appreciate the advice, but I'm content with my life as it is. Not everyone can be blissfully happy doing what they love all the time."

"Why not? You asked me why I didn't work with animals and went into childcare instead. Well, I'll tell you. I really like working with children. I knew I didn't have the stomach for working with animals. But I also love kids, and kids have always loved me. I could make a lot more money doing something else, but I wouldn't get a million hugs a day from a bunch of people who say that Miss Nicole is their very best friend in the whole wide world."

But what would Miss Nicole do if she'd made a stupid mistake when she was younger and had a felony on her record? No school would hire her. Nicole was fortunate that her wise choices over the years enabled her to do the things she loved.

Fernando didn't have that luxury. He was doing the best he could with what he had, and it had to be enough.

"I don't see why you can't even just try," Nicole continued. "There's no harm in asking about horse training jobs just to see what's available. The dude ranch that Erin works for as an accountant hires wranglers to come in every summer to help with their horses."

Her earnest tone made it almost impossible to refuse. Except he knew more about the business than she did. It wasn't like he hadn't tried working with horses when he got out.

"That's a seasonal job. What happens in the winter, when people aren't coming out to play cowboy? I'm sure he hires college kids to work in the summer and then they go back to school. I've looked at operations like that before. That's how it works."

One of his jobs after he'd gotten out had been at such a ranch. But one of the girls who worked there had had a crush on him, and he didn't return her feelings. Somehow, she'd found out about his record, and told her boss that she wasn't comfortable working with a felon. It had been enough for the guy to apologetically tell Fernando he had to let him go. If that girl could so easily get rid of him, who else would hurt him when they knew about his past?

Because that was the thing. People thought they knew. They didn't. He'd met a lot of guys in prison that he wouldn't turn his back on for anything, because he knew what kind of men they were. But there were other guys, guys like him, who'd made some bad choices but were committed to living a good life now.

"You don't know that's how Ricky works," Nicole insisted. "You should at least ask."

Fernando shook his head. "No. And now let's be done with this conversation. You need to respect my wishes and stay out of it."

He inclined his head over to Snookie, who was beginning to show signs of impatience as she pawed at the ground. "She doesn't like having to wait on us, and even though I don't want to continue this conversation, us standing around talking, ignoring her, is good for her. Just another way of showing her that we are the boss. Not her."

Nicole looked thoughtful for a moment. "So what are we supposed to do? Just keep making her wait?"

He nodded. "I want to see how far we can push her."

Nicole made an irritated noise. "I just don't know why you won't—" Then she stopped. "All right. But what else can we talk about? You don't want to talk about your future, and we've probably already talked too much about the past. So what else is there?"

"How about those Rockies?"

She gave him a funny look. "You follow baseball?"

"Nope. But isn't that what people talk about when they don't want to talk about other things? The sports team?"

Nicole rewarded him with a smile, and he thought again about how much he liked her. Even though it had been annoying, all her questions about his training, he knew it came from a place of compassion and caring. There was so much to like about Nicole, he just couldn't give her the answers she wanted.

"Do you think we're crazy for wanting to have our own ranch?" she asked. "People in town do, and I think Shane kind of does. I don't really remember coming here when we were kids, at least not like my sisters do. But my whole life, I always thought I wanted to live in a place like this with a bunch of animals, so maybe there's a part of that memory inside me subconsciously."

Fernando shrugged. "I don't think it's crazy. I wouldn't mind a place like this myself. But I don't have any long-lost relative to give me one. I'll work hard for my uncle, save up some money, and maybe someday I can get a place. It will be smaller, but it will be mine."

She gave him a thoughtful look. "I guess that makes sense. At least you have a plan. I never had much of one, in terms of getting animals. Until we got this ranch, I was kind of adrift. I had my job, and I loved it, but I always felt like something was missing. Being here, I know what I was meant to do."

He had that same feeling, except he knew it wouldn't last. But maybe someday.

Snookie calmed down again, giving him the break he wanted. "Notice Snookie's behavior. She's doing what we want."

Nicole reached over and patted Snookie. "Good girl," she said. "You're a very good girl."

He liked how Nicole automatically found moments to praise her horse. He could see why she was probably a very good teacher. She was patient and kind and quick to dole out praise and comfort. No wonder her students said that she was their best friend. She'd be a great mom, and he hoped someday she'd have a family of her own.

Though he had to admit the thought of it pained him more than he liked, knowing he wouldn't be part of it. Best to focus on easier things.

"Let's bring her in for the night," he said.

He let Nicole take the lead, and he liked the confidence in the way she handled her horse. He'd seen a lot of growth in both Snookie and Nicole over the past week, and he knew that no matter when he left, Nicole would be able to carry on his training and Snookie would be a great horse.

But he had to admit that sometimes when he allowed himself a few minutes of fancy, he did wonder, *what if?* What if he could find a way to stay? But that was crazy, and he was better off not thinking about it.

Chapter Nine

Nicole grabbed a cup of coffee and sat in the café, going over lesson plans while she waited for Janie to meet her.

Janie bustled in, looking as frazzled as ever. From what Nicole understood, Janie was not only working full-time while raising her son, but because her mother had cancer and was too ill to be out and about, Janie also helped with a lot of the things her mother did for her father's ministry.

"Sorry I'm late," Janie said. "We forgot Sam's shoes for soccer practice, so we had to run back home. I have to leave in a bit to pick him up, but I thought we could at least have a little time before I have to go."

Once Della, the owner, had taken their orders, Nicole smiled at Janie. "I'm so glad you invited me to coffee. I've been wanting to get to know people in our group better, but I'm not sure where to start."

Janie smiled. "I'm sure you'll find everyone is nice. I've known most of them my whole life, and I'm grateful for their friendship."

Maybe someday Nicole could say the same thing. But right now, it felt awkward sitting in the coffee shop with Janie.

"I'm just going to cut right to the chase," Janie said. "You might remember that my mother has cancer. Though everyone is praying for her healing, the doctor sat down with me and Dad last week and told us there's nothing more he can do. We discussed it as a family, and we've decided that rather than continuing with treatment that's only making Mom miserable, we're stopping treatment and letting her die in peace and dignity. We just want to make her last days as good as they can be."

Nicole reached out and took the other woman's hands. "I am so sorry. This must be difficult for you, considering all the times you've asked us to pray for your family. Is there anything I can do?"

Janie smiled at Nicole as she nodded. "That's why I wanted to talk to you. How do I explain to my son that his grandma is going to die? How do I make that okay? How do I help him grieve?"

Della brought their coffees and bear claws, so Nicole took the time to fix her coffee the way she liked it to give thought to Janie's questions.

"That's a hard one," Nicole said. "But why are you asking me? I teach preschool. Sam is Dylan's age."

Janie looked up from the bear claw she was picking at. "I know, but you're good with kids of all ages. Monica Rivers told me that you were really helpful when she needed to explain her divorce to her children. I just thought maybe you would have some wisdom for me.

Plus, you had some great insight in our Bible study yesterday."

The discouragement in Janie's voice made her heart hurt.

"That was really nice of Monica to say. I just did my best and listened. I think a lot of times, the reason these life events are so hard on kids is because it's unknown. We do so much trying to make it good for the kids that we forget to just be honest. That's what your son needs more than anything."

As they continued to talk, and Janie shared her burdens, she could see the relief on the other woman's face. Nicole couldn't help thinking that even though her situation had been different, she was a lot like Janie.

Her advice about being honest was mostly just what Nicole wished others would do for her.

Janie's phone beeped, and Janie looked down at it. "That means I need to go get Sam. I'm sorry this was all about me this time, but I hope we can do this again. I'd like to get to know you better as well."

"That would be great," Nicole said. "I've been realizing recently that we need to do more to share our burdens with others because we're only as alone in our struggles as we allow ourselves to be."

A hard truth, especially because the idea of trusting anyone was still so difficult.

Janie gave her a smile. "I'd like to agree, but it's tough for me, being the pastor's daughter. Even though we're very up-front in admitting that we're not perfect, it seems like people don't want to hear that we're human, too."

Nicole smiled at her. "Well, you can be human with

me whenever you want. I need to do a better job of being human with others, too. This was a good start for both of us."

Maybe Nicole wasn't the only one with trust issues. And if Janie could trust Nicole, then maybe Nicole could find a way to start trusting as well.

Janie smiled. "It's just really hard, always having to do the right thing all the time."

Then she stopped and pulled a paper out of her purse. "I almost forgot again. Last week, when he was hurrying out of church, Fernando dropped this. I tried to catch him yesterday, but he'd left already. I meant to give it to you, but I forgot. Can you see that he gets it?"

As Janie held out the paper, Nicole felt a little sick. It was the supply list Fernando had said he'd forgotten—the one Nicole had thought he'd been lying about.

Fernando hadn't lied, but Nicole, with her grudge against him, had assumed he had. Not that she'd actually accused him, because then he'd have presented her with his own version of the events. She probably wouldn't have believed him, so it once again pointed to the idea that perhaps the real problem wasn't with Fernando, but with Nicole, and her heart.

Nicole took the paper and stared down at it. She owed Fernando an apology, but she didn't even know where to start.

As Nicole got up to leave, Erin entered the café, along with her boss, Ricky.

"Nicole," Erin said, smiling. "What are you doing here?"

"I just had coffee with Janie. Thanks to some of my conversations with Fernando, I've realized that I haven't been doing a very good job of trying to make friends here."

A wide smile filled Ricky's face. "You've got lots of friends. I'm your friend. In fact, if you're ever looking for a boyfriend, you should consider me. I do miss having myself a girlfriend."

The old man had to be at least eighty; those in town said he was close to a hundred. Ricky's wife had passed long before the sisters had come to town, and though everyone told them that Ricky loved his wife deeply, he was also the town's biggest flirt.

"I'll keep that in mind," Nicole said. "If I ever decide to get a boyfriend, I'll definitely call you first."

Erin shook her head as she looked over Ricky. "Don't hold your breath. I've seen the way Nicole looks at Fernando, and the way he looks at her, and I'm pretty sure we're going to be hearing another set of wedding bells in the future."

Ricky looked over at Erin. "Fernando? Is that the horse trainer you said you girls hired?"

Erin nodded. "He is. And you wouldn't believe what a great job he's doing."

Ricky nodded thoughtfully. "You should tell him to give me a call. I had to let my trainer go because he kept showing up to work inebriated. My horses are too valuable to be handled by some drunk."

Then he turned to Nicole. "This trainer of yours drink?"

"No," Nicole said. "But I'm not sure he's interested in another training job. He's got a construction job with his uncle waiting, and he doesn't want to let him down."

It seemed right to tell Ricky the reason Fernando had

given for not looking at training jobs. It also felt wrong not to give Fernando an opportunity at his dream.

Maybe this was how she could make it up to Fernando.

"To be honest," Nicole continued, "I think Fernando is worried about accepting a horse training position because he said that kind of work is feast or famine and he wants steady work."

Ricky nodded thoughtfully. "He has a point. A lot of guys go into business as a trainer, thinking it will be easy, only to realize there are a lot of things they hadn't considered. But right now, I've got a string of seventy-five horses to accommodate our guests on the ranch, and I need someone full-time. If your friend comes to work for me, it will be steady work."

The job seemed almost perfect. "Fernando was saying that a lot of guest ranches only have seasonal jobs for the people dealing with animals. Is that true of your ranch?"

Ricky made a disgusted noise. "I've got families coming in the summer, hunters during hunting season, people wanting sleigh rides in the winter when they're bored with skiing and lots of folks in between. Even if things weren't going as well, and we didn't have guests year-round, the horses would get ornery if you only worked with them part of the year."

The old man laughed, like he'd just told himself a great joke. It was kind of funny, if you thought about it. Even if Ricky didn't have guests, he'd still need people to work the horses.

"It sounds like a great opportunity for the right person," Nicole said.

Erin nodded. "It is. I'm sure you know how happy I am, working for Ricky, and I think it would be a good job for anyone."

Then Erin turned to Ricky. "Leah has been wanting to have you over for dinner for a while anyway, so why don't you come over tomorrow night? You can meet Fernando, and you guys can talk to see if applying for your job would be a good fit for him. Shane seems to think the world of him, and honestly, I think we all like him. Plus, I want you to see what he's done with Snookie."

Ricky made a strangled noise in the back of his throat. "That stubborn mare I said was only good for dog food?"

It pained Nicole to hear Snookie talked about like that, but it wasn't the first she'd heard that term being used. Still, it felt good to know what they had accomplished.

"The same," Nicole said. "I'm glad I didn't listen to everyone who told me to give up on her. Fernando says she's going to be a good horse."

"I'll believe that when I see it," Ricky muttered. "But if he can turn that horse around, I definitely want him on my team."

His vote of confidence warmed Nicole's heart. Working for Ricky sounded like it had real promise for Fernando. Could she convince Fernando to give his dream a chance? Because of him, Nicole had found a deeper healing in her life and was starting to have a greater hope for her future. Perhaps making this connection with Ricky would give Fernando the same.

Her sisters had been right in thinking that Nicole

and Fernando needed each other for their healing. The question was, would Fernando be open to it as well?

Fernando was just putting the finishing touches on the tile of the apartment kitchen when he heard a knock at his door. He stepped back, pleased with his progress. It was nice he'd have someone to show it off to.

He opened the door to find Nicole standing there, a wide grin filling her face.

"Guess what?" she asked, stepping into his apartment before he could invite her in.

"Come in. What's going on?"

She waved off his attempt to get her to sit. "I can't stay. Leah needs me to help her clean house for tomorrow night."

Her wide grin made him want to smile, too. "What's tomorrow night?"

Seeing her happy, especially since it wasn't often he saw her this excited, made his heart swell with joy.

"Erin's boss, Ricky, is coming to dinner, and he wants to meet you," she said. "He's looking for a new horse trainer. We mentioned you, and he was excited to hear about your work with Snookie. Leah has been wanting to have him over anyway, so this is perfect."

He started to open his mouth to explain to her just how much he didn't appreciate her interference. But she was so excited, and she didn't have all the facts. Facts he still wasn't sure he wanted her to have.

"Oh no," she said. "I know that look. You're going to argue with me and tell me how impractical it is or how a dude ranch isn't ideal. But let me tell you. He said this is a full-time job. He has a string of over seventy-five horses that need work year-round. You would be perfect."

No, he wouldn't. Not with his record.

"I told you, I already have a job with my uncle."

Nicole made a noise. "You would honestly rather work for your uncle, doing a job you don't love, for what has to be a pathetically low wage, when you could be working with horses? Sorry, but that's crazy. And you can't say it's about family loyalty. I know the uncle you're talking about. Adriana said he was a jerk and a cheapskate."

She looked at him expectantly, but he didn't have an answer. She was right. What was he supposed to say?

"You should at least talk to Ricky," Nicole said. "I'll admit I don't know all the details, but Erin loves working for him, and he's done so much for our family out of the kindness of his heart. You should have seen all the Christmas presents he bought the boys. He's a really great person, and I know you'll love meeting him. Come to dinner tomorrow night, and you can see for yourself."

Why couldn't she have just given up on her crazy idea and let him be?

"I can't," he said finally.

Nicole plopped down on his couch. "Why not? And don't tell me it's because you have other plans. You don't have plans. You have no friends in this town, and you haven't tried to get to know anyone. When you come to church, you sit in the back, come in late and leave early so you don't have to talk to anyone. What's with you?"

He didn't think she'd noticed. He'd actually hoped to slip in and out of church without anyone noticing. But so far, that plan was failing miserably.

He looked up at the fridge, where one of the magnets held up the flyer for all the church activities. So tempting…but no.

"I just don't think it's a good idea to get involved in a church that I'm not going to be around for in a few weeks," he finally said. "It's not fair to them or me."

Nicole looked up at him, a childlike expression on her face. "You could be if you wanted to. What's this really about?"

He hadn't thought that Nicole would take his decision personally, but as he looked at the sadness in her eyes, he realized that's exactly what happened.

He sat down beside her. "It's complicated," he said. "I don't want to hurt you, but you need to understand that there's a lot more going on here. And you have to trust me that this is for the best."

The expression on her face was like he'd just told her he wasn't going to help with Snookie anymore. That was crazy. What did it matter to her? She hated him. Okay, so she didn't. She'd already said as much. And they'd definitely come to a place of forgiveness and understanding. He just hadn't realized that in making peace with Nicole, he would make it harder on her for him to leave.

The look she gave him wasn't one of trust, but one of concern. "I know I've been difficult. But I wanted to explain, and to apologize."

She pulled a piece of paper out of her pocket and handed it to him. When he looked at it, he realized it was the list he'd lost.

"I've been upset with you," she said. "When you said you didn't want to ride with us to church because you had errands to run, and I saw you at home, having clearly not run any errands, I thought you'd lied to me. I was hurt and angry, because it took a lot for me to open up to you about my faith and invite you to church."

The dejected expression on her face made his heart hurt. He hadn't realized that by not participating with her in church, it would cause so much damage. After that first Sunday, he'd known she was upset, but it hadn't occurred to him just how deeply she'd be wounded.

"The fact that you'd lied to me told me you hadn't changed. You'd obviously lied to me before, with Adriana and Brandon, and this was proof that I still couldn't trust you. I'm sorry. I believed the worst of you when I should have just asked you and not jumped to conclusions."

Though he knew her apology was meant to clear the air between them, it only made him feel worse.

"Thanks," he said. "But I don't deserve your apology. No, I didn't lie, but I was looking for excuses not to spend time with you at church. I'm sorry. I should have just told you that while I did want to go to church, I didn't want to get involved. Instead, I made up excuses. You were right to mistrust me."

His confession didn't make him feel any better. Especially since it made the pained expression on Nicole's face even worse.

"But why?" she asked.

He couldn't give her the answer she wanted. Not when he would love to stay and build a life here. But built on the foundation of his record, it would be like building on sand.

They were silent for a moment, then Nicole straightened her back and looked over at him. "I get it. I'm sorry," she said. "I know I've made you uncomfortable a few times because…"

She hesitated and looked dejected again. Then she let out a long sigh. "I'm not sure why I'm attracted to you. Except that it's more than just how good-looking you are. I mean, yes, you are. But you're such a good man, and you've been so kind and patient with me, as well as with my horse. If it's any consolation, I'm trying not to have feelings for you, because it's obvious you don't return them and I don't even know what this is."

She looked like she was about to cry. He couldn't help himself. He pulled her close to him and kissed her gently.

How could she think he didn't want her? Sometimes it was all he thought about, wanting her. For all the same reasons she'd just described about wanting him.

But just as soon as he kissed her, he knew what a terrible mistake he'd made. Kissing her only made him want her more. And it only made the pain in his heart at the inevitable even worse.

He pulled away and looked at her. Her face was flushed, her lips puffy, and her eyes were shining. She looked like a woman who'd been kissed by a man she loved. And he was about to break her heart.

"Don't ever think that I don't feel the same way. I do, and that's exactly why those fleeting moments have been so uncomfortable for me. We can't be together. You need to know that now and accept it as reality. It's sweet that you're trying to keep me here, but I can't stay. I'm no good for you."

He watched the various expressions play across her

face as she shook her head slowly. "If it's because of our past history…"

"It's not. None of this has anything to do with you. It's about me. And my past."

The confusion on her face brought an ache to his heart. She'd already been through so much, and he hated how difficult he was making things for her.

"Then what?" she asked. "You don't have a secret wife or something, do you? Adriana said you went away for a while to find yourself, but that was before I knew you, so I don't know anything about that. But it can't be so terrible that we can't work through whatever it is. It's not like I'm asking you to marry me or anything, but we should at least explore what's going on between us."

He figured he'd end up having to tell her the truth at some point, but he hadn't expected it to be this hard. Fernando took a deep breath and asked for the words he needed.

"I didn't go find myself," he said. "I was in prison. My family was ashamed of me and what I'd done, so they made it sound like I was off on some youthful lark when in reality, I was behind bars."

She stared at him like she couldn't process his words. But she had to learn to accept the reality. His reality. And the reason they couldn't be together.

"It's true," he said. "I spent seven years in prison. Federal prison. It's where I learned to train horses. They get mustangs from the Bureau of Land Management and they give them to prisoners to train as part of their rehabilitation program. I'm sure it was one of the best things that ever happened to me, even if I didn't recognize it at the time."

She gave him a funny look. "I don't understand what that has to do with us."

Had she not understood what he'd just said?

"I told you, I went to prison. I'm a convicted felon. We don't have a future together."

"What did you do?" Nicole asked.

He'd been a little surprised Adriana hadn't told her, since Adriana had told him that she hated him for ruining her life by going to prison. He'd have figured that she'd tell her best friend all about it, but apparently, her shame over Fernando's actions was too great for even that.

"I was convicted of being an accomplice to a robbery in which a lady was killed," he said.

The wide-eyed look she gave him was exactly what he would have expected. But he didn't want to sugarcoat things to make it sound like he wasn't accepting responsibility for his role in the situation.

"That doesn't sound like something you'd do. I can't see you being part of something like that."

Her faith in him was surprising, even though she'd just admitted having feelings for him. His own mother called him a murderer, even though the prosecution admitted there was nothing tying him to the lady's death—just driving the getaway car.

But somehow he wanted to maintain Nicole's faith in him, even though he knew at the end of this, he'd have to let her go. What else was he supposed to do? Beyond all hope, she'd gone from hating his guts to caring about him, and even though it felt good to have the attention, he knew that staying with him would ruin her life.

What happened if they did end up together, married,

creating a life together? And then he got fired from the job supporting them because someone was uncomfortable with his record? What happened when someone accused him of stealing and people believed it because they found out what he'd been convicted of in the past?

All things that had happened since his release, things that seemed innocuous to most people, but were capable of ruining not just his life, but that of the ones he loved.

He needed Nicole to understand the truth.

"I didn't know I was helping out in a robbery," he said. "My buddy Mike started hanging out with a bad crowd. I don't have any idea why he thought he had to impress those guys, but it became an obsession with him."

He looked at Nicole, hoping she'd understand where he was coming from. "I did everything I could to warn him, but he wouldn't listen."

Nicole nodded slowly, like she was processing his words. "How did that turn into a robbery?"

"Mike called one night, frantic, because something bad happened. He wouldn't say what. He asked me to pick him up, and to hurry."

Even now, looking back, he wouldn't have said no. There was no way he could have known what Mike had done. A friend was in trouble, and he'd thought it was just a ride.

"I met him at a park. When he got in the car, he was freaking out. These guys he got involved with had asked him to prove himself by robbing this lady. But it all went wrong, and the lady was home, and she had a gun. There was a struggle with one of the guys, and the gun went off, killing her. The other guys left, leaving

Mike there by himself. He ran, ending up in the park, where he called me."

Nicole made a sympathetic noise, and though he expected her to have the same judgmental expression on her face others had when he described his crime, she seemed more...open.

"It probably would have turned out differently, but the cops pulled me over less than a mile away for an expired tag on Adriana's car. I'd taken hers, not knowing that the reason she'd borrowed mine was because she needed new tags. They immediately recognized Mike as being the robbery suspect, so they searched my car. The stolen items were in his backpack on my back seat. Which made me an accomplice."

As he told the story, he'd walked over to the window and looked out. The open space made him feel less confined after having been trapped, not just in a physical prison, but in a mental one.

Nicole came to stand beside him. "Why didn't you tell the police you were innocent?"

"I was a Mexican in a rich white neighborhood. Those cops weren't going to listen. I figured I'd use my right to remain silent, talk to an attorney and then everything would be sorted out."

Which was the logical response. Only that hadn't been what happened. He turned to look at Nicole.

"When I got to jail, my mom refused to take the call. The police said I'd have to wait until the next morning to get a public defender. That first night, one of the guys in my cell got a message to me from the ringleader. If I told anyone what I knew, they'd go after my family."

He could still feel the fear of having that man's hands on him, his foul breath and the whispered threats.

"He mentioned Adriana by name."

The shock on Nicole's face made him feel better about his decision. She'd do anything for her sisters, and their conversation had made her realize that his love for Adriana had been no different.

"So I didn't say anything about what I knew of the crime. I told my public defender that a friend called and needed a ride, so I picked him up. Told them I didn't know anything else. I couldn't prove that I didn't know. The DA knew I was innocent. That was the crazy thing. He told me if I just named names, they would drop all charges against me."

Nicole looked at him like he'd been crazy not to take the deal. But she didn't understand. No one did, especially since he'd been too afraid to tell anyone the rest. But Nicole had shared a very deep part of herself with him, and it seemed wrong not to be completely open with her.

"My family was getting threats, so I said nothing. They all thought it was because the media was all over the story and people wanted to punish me for killing a poor, innocent lady. My lawyer negotiated a plea, and I took it. It was better than going to trial and being convicted of murder."

Nicole nodded slowly. "You went to prison to get them to leave your family alone."

"Exactly. But no one knew that. My family was humiliated. They didn't know the full story, and honestly, no one cares. They see the conviction on my record, and that's all that matters."

He opened the window and looked out at the open space of the ranch. He'd never take this ability for granted again. Even though there was sympathy on her face, he wondered if he should have told her. The truth meant he wasn't the hardened criminal his conviction said he was, but she also didn't understand what his silence had cost him.

Nicole moved closer to him. "Thank you for trusting me."

The look on her face meant that she was going to try to hug him or offer him some comfort. But comfort wouldn't erase the conviction on his record or make it any easier for him to be with her.

He stepped away and crossed his arms over his chest.

"Why do you think that means I wouldn't want to be with you?" she asked.

Fernando tried not to groan. He probably should've had this conversation with her before he'd kissed her. Having admitted their feelings only muddied the waters and prevented her from seeing the truth.

"You won't have a normal life with me," he said. "You want to know why I can't get a decent job? Why I'm forced to work with my uncle? It's because no one wants to hire a felon. I had a job working with horses, and guess what? Even though my boss didn't have a problem with it, my coworkers did. I've been on jobs where something went missing and the finger was always pointed at me, even though I hadn't done it. All anyone saw was that I had a theft on my record, and I was presumed guilty. Add in the fact that a lady died? They were all sure I'd kill them in their beds."

No one had ever charged him with other crimes, but

he'd always been offered the opportunity to leave quietly and no charges would be filed. After being railroaded so easily before, he'd never been willing to take the risk of defending himself.

"I didn't need to hear all the facts of your story to know you couldn't have stolen anything," Nicole said. "You're not the sort of person who would take anything from anyone, let alone kill someone."

He stared at her for a moment. "And what sort of person would? Because honestly, I don't know anymore how you would tell. Some of the worst men I knew in prison were the kind who seemed like the nicest guy on the planet. But some of the best men I knew looked like the hardest criminal."

Nicole came over to him and put her arm around him. "It's not about what you look like, but the kind of man you are. You put up with my hatred, and you are so patient with Snookie. It's not in your character."

Her faith in him made his heart hurt worse than it had at any other point in his ordeal.

"That's kind of you to say, but not even my own mother believed that of me."

"But I'm not your mother," Nicole said, looking up at him with an expression that made him think she was going to try to kiss him. If he bent down, even the slightest, they'd kiss again.

And as much as he wanted to, he couldn't ruin her life.

"I'm not the man you need me to be," he said, turning away. "You've already wasted your heart on a man who didn't deserve it. Don't make the same mistake again."

She made a choked noise, like his words had

wounded her. He hadn't wanted to hurt her, but she'd given him no other choice. Fernando might not have been the same kind of pig Brandon had been. But that was the point. He wasn't selfish enough to take the heart of someone who deserved far better.

Fortunately, she didn't continue arguing with him. She walked away, and it wasn't until he heard the door close behind her that he let himself relax.

He just prayed that if Nicole ever did fall in love with someone, that man would be worthy of her love. And he also prayed that someday, he could pray that prayer without it absolutely gutting him.

Chapter Ten

Fernando didn't show. Nicole looked out the kitchen window at the barn. She'd knocked on his apartment door a while ago, and not only had he not answered, but the door had been locked. He hadn't literally put out a sign that said, "go away," but he might as well have.

Fine. Message received.

Fernando wasn't interested in taking a chance on his own future, and even though it hurt Nicole to realize that he wasn't willing to do it for her, she'd accept his decision. Though she hadn't forced Brandon into their engagement, the more she thought about the weeks and months leading to him leaving her at the altar, the more she realized just how much he'd checked out. At the time, she'd chalked it up to him being busy at work and nerves, but now she knew better.

It had taken until now, and working with Fernando on Snookie, to make her realize that forcing her agenda didn't work out so well for her. She was done pushing, and if Fernando wanted to waste his talent on a job he didn't love for a guy who wouldn't appreciate him, that was his choice. And it was his choice to not even give their relationship a chance. If he couldn't value her enough to fight for her, then fine. She deserved better.

Even if it made her feel sick to her stomach to think about it.

Shane came up behind her. "Have you talked to Fernando? I can't find him anywhere. Did you tell him about dinner with Ricky?"

Nicole sighed as she turned to face him. "He's not interested."

"That's crazy," Leah said, joining them. "Why not?"

Because Fernando was an idiot, but that didn't exactly sound like the best answer to give. Especially since she wanted to protect his privacy.

Not that her family would care about his record, because once they heard his story, they'd be as sympathetic as she was. But he seemed so ashamed of it, it felt wrong for her to be the one to tell them if he was choosing to keep it a secret.

"You'll have to ask him," Nicole said, brushing past them and into the living room, where Ricky was regaling the boys with tales of being a cowboy and riding the range.

"I need to go check on Snookie," she said, knowing it was rude to leave now but needing some space to have a quick cry.

Even though Fernando had told her he wouldn't come, part of her had hoped that he'd have a change of heart. She'd prayed that God would help him realize the truth about his past and that people would see his heart for what it was.

But that was the trouble with praying for things.

Sometimes you got what you wanted, and other times you just ended up with a broken heart. And though it was easy to want to say that was the whole reason she didn't like praying anyway, she thought about what Fernando had said about prayer—that the point was having faith and believing that God was good and had their best interests in mind.

Fine, then.

She'd believe God knew what He was doing, even if it meant that once again, the little hope Nicole had of happiness was gone. She wasn't going to push for her own agenda anymore.

At least she had Snookie.

Nicole went into the barn and over to Snookie's stall, where the horse was happily munching on some hay.

"Hey, girl," Nicole said, reaching in to pet the horse. "See? This is why I said you were my only love. You're the only one who's not going to leave me and break my heart. Why bother trusting and opening up when you're still going to end up alone in the end?"

Snookie whinnied, and Nicole let herself into the stall. Snookie turned and nudged her like she understood Nicole needed her comfort.

"Thanks, girl. Even though Fernando doesn't want me, you do, don't you?"

The horse laid her head on Nicole's shoulder, the way she'd done when they'd joined up, and Nicole put her arms around Snookie's neck.

"I love you, Snookie."

The tears that fell weren't unexpected. After all, that's why Nicole had come in here in the first place. But rather than feeling relief, Nicole only felt worse.

It was so unfair.

Not just Fernando's unwillingness to give their relationship a chance, or that he'd refused to even talk to Ricky to see what Ricky thought of his record. But even the injustice of Fernando's conviction and how he'd been punished for doing what had come naturally to him—helping a friend.

How could someone with such a good heart spend his life suffering for his actions? Wasn't going to prison supposed to be penalty enough? He'd paid his debt to society and yet he was still being punished.

As she held the horse, sobbing, Nicole felt a weird prick at her shoulder. She lifted her head and realized what had just happened.

Snookie had bitten her.

"Snookie!" Nicole jumped away, and Snookie reared.

In seconds, the horse had gone from being calm to being more agitated than Nicole had seen her in a while.

But why?

This wasn't like her horse at all. At least not since Fernando had begun training her.

Snookie reared again, and Nicole quickly exited the stall. As she worked the latch shut, a searing pain shot through her shoulder. She grabbed her shoulder with her other hand, and it was damp. When she pulled her hand away and looked at it, it was covered in blood. Snookie must've bitten her harder than she thought.

Despite the pain in her shoulder, the greater pain was in the pit of her stomach. When Shane found out, he was going to be upset. No, not upset. Livid.

Nicole went to the small bathroom in the back of the

barn to survey the damage. Maybe it was one of those flesh wounds that bled a lot but wasn't really bad.

But when she twisted in front of the mirror, she saw that the damage was worse than she'd thought. Who knew a horse bite could be so bad?

Fortunately, they kept some bandages in the cabinet, as well as some antibiotic ointment.

She should go into the house and get one of her sisters to help her clean the wound, but as she imagined the expressions on their faces, she couldn't get her feet to move.

Shane's threat rang in her head. If Snookie bit one more person, he'd make Nicole get rid of her. And a bite this bad? There'd be no pleading her way out of it, especially since Leah always deferred to him when it came to the animals.

Nicole did her best to put pressure on the wound, weighing her options. If she could clean things up herself, Shane would never know. She'd figure out why Snookie bit her and buy some more time to help her horse. Surely there was something in the books about what had happened. How to fix it.

She finished cleaning the wound, a difficult task since she couldn't quite reach the back of her shoulder where she'd been bitten, but at least the bleeding had stopped. Once she bandaged it, she felt a little better. Yes, it hurt, but she'd be okay.

Once Nicole got herself fixed up, she cleaned up her mess so there was no sign of the incident. Her shirt, however, was another story.

But if she remembered correctly, they had a few old

work shirts in the tack room. She could change into one and hopefully no one would notice.

Nicole quickly changed and hid the bloody shirt behind some tools. She'd come back for it later. They were probably missing her in the house.

When she reentered the house, her sisters and Shane were laughing at one of Ricky's stories. She could hear the boys playing in the other room. No one appeared to have missed her. At least that was something going right with the evening. Especially since her shoulder was starting to throb.

"How's Snookie?" Erin asked as soon as Ricky was done with his story.

Nicole forced a smile on her face. "Fine. I always have such a hard time leaving her."

"I'd have liked to have seen that trainer of yours work with her," Ricky said. "When do you expect him back? I haven't had any decent applicants to my job posting, so maybe I can convince him to come on board."

How Ricky would convince him, she wasn't sure. But he could try. Maybe Ricky could say something that would make a difference.

"I don't know," Nicole said. "He seems pretty set on going to work for his uncle."

Leah made a disgusted noise. "Why would he want to work in construction when he could be training horses full-time? It doesn't make sense. I've seen him working on projects around here, but he doesn't seem as happy doing it as he is when he's working with Snookie."

Funny that even her sister noticed it.

"He's a good worker," Shane said. "But you're right. He's an even better horse trainer. I don't get it, either.

I'll have a word with him. Maybe he didn't understand the situation. He'd be a fool to not at least talk to Ricky and see what it's about."

As her family discussed the merits of Fernando working with Ricky, Nicole's heart ached at the idea of Fernando missing out. Would hearing their praise make a difference in his decision? Did he understand what everyone thought of him? But would that even matter? Or was the label he'd been given too deeply ingrained in him for him to overcome?

Nicole took a deep breath. "What are the qualifications for the job? What do you look for in a candidate? What would make you not hire someone?"

As Ricky listed what he wanted in a trainer, he never mentioned anything about a person's criminal record. It was on the tip of her tongue to ask, but she didn't want to be too specific, in case it gave away Fernando's secret.

But maybe it was better that she stay out of it. She didn't know what to think of anything anymore. She'd thought they were making progress with Snookie, and out of the blue, Snookie had bitten her. At least the boys knew to stay away from the horse. She just had to figure out what had made Snookie bite this time, and how to prevent it in the future.

Honestly, though, she was stumped.

But could she even confide in Fernando?

He was already upset with her for trying to set up a meeting with Ricky. And even though he'd said he'd do whatever it took to help Nicole with Snookie, what would he say when he found out what had happened in the barn?

Maybe Nicole wasn't meant to have anyone—or

anything—to love. It seemed like every time she thought she was close, something happened to destroy it. Brandon could have had a great life with her, but he chose to throw it away by running off with Adriana. Fernando could have had a great job as a horse trainer, where he could have explored his feelings for Nicole, but he'd chosen to let the fear of his past keep him away. And then there was Snookie… Maybe Nicole had been foolish to think that she could fix her broken horse.

So what dreams were left for Nicole?

Fernando stared at his phone after his conversation with his uncle. While Uncle Sergio had initially told him the job wasn't starting right away, he was now demanding that Fernando either be at work on Monday or find himself another job.

Given that it was Friday morning, that meant he only had three more days to help Snookie. There was no way Snookie would be fully ready in three days, even if he worked nonstop.

Granted, Salida was only a couple of hours away, so maybe Fernando could still come over on weekends to help, but it wouldn't give the horse the same consistency she needed.

But what other option did he have?

He glanced out the window and watched Nicole's car pull out of the driveway to take her to work. Nicole would tell him to talk to this Ricky person and see about that job.

Did she realize how unfair it was to see his dream dangled before him, knowing how easily it could be taken away?

Sighing, Fernando cleaned up his breakfast dishes. He'd go down to the barn and reassess Snookie. Come up with a set of exercises for Nicole to give Snookie during the week, and every weekend, he'd drive back to check their progress and see what needed to be tweaked. Hopefully, it would be enough. It had to be enough.

When he went downstairs, the barn was quiet. Peaceful. Exactly the way he liked it. Except Snookie seemed more agitated than usual. She'd been acting up all week, and he couldn't figure out why.

"What's up, girl?"

Snookie pawed at the ground.

He grabbed her hay and tossed it into her stall, hoping the food would calm her down. And though Snookie immediately began eating, her posture was still more tense than usual.

While Snookie ate, Fernando went into the tack room to gather the things he needed for training today. Maybe she hadn't been worked hard enough lately. He'd cut their time short on Monday in case Ricky showed up early. If Ricky had arrived while he was working with Snookie, he'd have ended up being forced to go to dinner and talk to the man about a job he desperately wanted but knew he couldn't accept.

Things had been off all week since, and Nicole had been even more distant as well. Maybe it was because she was finally accepting that they couldn't be together and realizing that the reality of what their life together would be like wasn't as great as it seemed.

Inside the tack room, Fernando noticed a stack of buckets had been moved.

When he went to pick them up, he saw a wadded-up ball of something in the corner. Odd. He kept the tack room immaculate, not only to make it easier to find things, but also to prevent critters from being attracted to the space. Hopefully the boys hadn't come in here to play.

He grabbed the item, and as soon as he had it in the light, he felt sick. It was a shirt. A bloody shirt. And, as he took a look at it, he knew exactly whose shirt it was. Nicole's.

How had her shirt gotten covered in blood, and what was it doing in the barn?

But as he examined it, and the tear in the shoulder, he had a pretty good guess. Snookie liked to nudge Nicole in the shoulder, so if the horse was in a particularly frisky mood, she could have bitten Nicole by accident. Only, since horses tended to clamp down hard on things, especially when playing, it would have been a bad bite. And it was, judging by the amount of blood on the shirt.

A shadow blocked the light from the doorway.

"Fernando?"

Shane.

If Snookie had bitten Nicole, and Shane found out, it would be the end of Snookie's time here. But Fernando didn't have all the facts. And it wouldn't be fair to discuss the situation with Shane without having talked to Nicole first.

Fernando wadded up the shirt as tightly as he could in his hand before turning to face Shane.

"What's up?"

"Why did you skip out on dinner the other night? Didn't Nicole tell you that the dinner was just as much for your benefit as anything else?"

The other man sounded disappointed in him, and though Shane was close to Fernando's age, it felt like he was letting down a mentor.

Fernando sighed. "I told Nicole I wasn't interested in the job. It didn't seem fair to get Ricky's hopes up."

"It's a good job," Shane said. "You're a good trainer. Why wouldn't you be interested?"

He could see where, logically, it didn't make sense to someone who didn't know the full story. After all, that's why he'd finally told Nicole about his past.

But Shane wasn't Nicole.

And he wasn't falling in love with Shane.

So he didn't owe the other man anything.

Did he?

"Like I told Nicole, I have a job waiting for me. In fact, my uncle needs me to start on Monday."

Shane rubbed his chin. "And you'd rather do construction for your uncle than train horses?"

No. But he couldn't give Shane that answer.

"He's my uncle. He helped me when no one else would."

Reasons Fernando would do well to remember. Everyone else had pretty much given up on him, but at least Uncle Sergio was giving him a chance. Probably not a fair chance, but it would be enough to survive.

"What about Nicole and Snookie?"

Fernando knew the tone in the other man's voice. It was a protective older brother, making sure the sister he loved wasn't going to be hurt.

"I'm going to put together some exercises for them to do during the week. I'll be back on weekends to check progress and come up with a plan for the next week."

Shane looked at him like he thought it was a stupid plan. And while Fernando agreed it wasn't ideal, at least it would enable him to keep his promise to Nicole.

The shirt weighed heavily in his hands. He had to keep his promise to Nicole, especially if what he suspected about Snookie biting her was true.

"If you worked for Ricky, you could still work with Snookie every day, the way you have been."

Fernando took a deep breath. This whole family just couldn't let go of the idea.

"I can't go work for Ricky."

Shane gave him a hard stare. "Why not?"

"Look," Fernando said. "There are things in my past I'm not proud of. People won't like me working on a guest ranch."

His heart was heavy in his chest. He didn't want to admit, once again, the mistakes of his past. But at least now, if Shane found out and didn't want him around, it wouldn't be the end of the world. Not when he couldn't stay anyway. He'd figure out some other way to help Nicole and Snookie.

"Your record, you mean," Shane said, looking thoughtful.

Had Nicole told him? He hadn't told her to keep it a secret, but the time they'd shared had seemed so personal, so intimate. He hadn't expected her to tell anyone.

"How do you know about it?" he asked.

Shane snorted. "You think I'm going to let someone come stay on this ranch, with women and children I love, without running a background check on them? It's easy enough to do these days, so I'm not going to risk their safety by letting a stranger stay here."

Fernando could only stare at him. He'd known all along? "Why didn't you say anything?"

"What's there to say?" Shane shrugged. "The way I see it, you committed a crime, and you paid your debt to society. I'm familiar with the program you were in. Walt Cunningham is one of the best trainers I know. Most guys would kill to work with him, but..."

Shane chuckled as he shook his head. "I guess that's how people do get to work with him these days. Though you didn't kill anyone, so there's that."

It was kind of funny, if you thought about it. Only they didn't have murderers in the program. Just a lot of guys like him, who'd made a stupid mistake.

"Anyway," Shane continued. "Everyone in the horse training world has heard about Walt and his methods. I've met guys who've hired men who were in Walt's program, and they can't say enough good things about them. Why wouldn't you tell people that?"

Being in the program was supposed to be a selling point of Fernando's skills when he got out. The trouble was, no one realized what a strike having a felony record actually was.

"You don't think I tried?" Fernando asked. "Look, I've been through all this with Nicole. People might say they want a guy with my expertise, but in the end, all they see is someone who was convicted of a crime. And they're afraid I'm going to do it again."

"Are you?"

No one had asked him that before. Nicole had simply told him she didn't believe him capable of it and had left it at that. But something about Shane's frank question made him feel a little better about this conversation.

"Absolutely not. I know it sounds like I'm making excuses, but I didn't even do what I was convicted of."

Shane nodded. "I figured there was more to the story, and that you'd tell it if and when you were ready. We all have things in our pasts we're not proud of. But you can't let it define you."

He hesitated, then gave Fernando a sharp look. "And honestly, until now, I'd have never pegged you for a coward. You're so afraid of being judged that you won't let yourself live. You won't risk going after your dream job, and you won't risk letting an amazing woman love you."

"What do you know about that?" Fernando stared at him.

Shane made an exasperated noise. "Anyone with eyes can see it. You're crazy about Nicole, and she seems really happy when she's around you. I obviously haven't known her very long, but I've never seen that light in her eyes before. Leah says she's seeing a deep healing in Nicole thanks to you."

It was good to hear that Nicole was finding the peace she needed. But the thing no one seemed to understand was that he was leaving precisely because he cared about her. He wanted her to have the chance at a good life and a decent future. Why didn't anyone else see that?

"I'll still be here every weekend," Fernando said.

Shane shook his head. "I should move your things out to the chicken coop."

Then he shoved his hands in his pockets. "But I won't. Leah and her sisters would fail to see the fitting nature of the move. But I am putting you on notice. I don't want to see Nicole getting hurt."

He understood the threat, loud and clear. It was delivered with the same power as his words about Snookie.

"Don't you get it? That's what I've been trying to do. She deserves better than I can give her. But I think you know Nicole well enough to know by now that she's more stubborn than that mare of hers. I try to keep my distance, but she keeps pushing her way in. So what else am I supposed to do?"

Shane looked him up and down. "Talk to Ricky. At least hear him out and give him the chance to decide for himself if he wants to hire someone with your past—and your skills. You sell yourself short in thinking that your past is all you are."

Easy enough for him to say. But for Fernando to argue the point further and explain how it hadn't worked out for him before was only inviting more of the same. Shane didn't understand, because he hadn't lived it.

"I know who I am," Fernando said. "And I've experienced all the opportunities that have fallen through because of it. So let's agree to disagree, and instead figure out a way to help Nicole get this horse where she wants her."

"Fine," Shane said. "You're clearly not the man I thought you were. And you're right. Nicole deserves better."

The other man turned and left, letting his words hit Fernando like a punch he hadn't seen coming but knew he deserved. He just hadn't thought it would hurt this much.

He liked and respected Shane. And realizing he

couldn't be the man Shane wanted him to be was only one more way he'd let the people in his life down.

As he looked at the shirt in his hands, he prayed he wouldn't be letting Nicole and Snookie down as well. He'd already disappointed Shane, and knowing how protective Shane was of his loved ones, Shane wouldn't hesitate to get rid of the last remaining threats to their safety.

Snookie—and Fernando.

Chapter Eleven

The pain in her shoulder had been excruciating all day at work. Even though she wasn't sure if it helped or not, she'd been taking the maximum dose of ibuprofen just in case it was doing something. Anything to make the throbbing stop.

All Nicole wanted to do was go home and fall into bed. Maybe sleep would help. She never knew a horse bite could be so painful. Especially since it had been a few days since it had happened. Shouldn't it be healing by now?

But when she pulled into the driveway, Fernando stepped out of the barn and headed for her car, like he'd been waiting to talk to her.

He probably had some new lesson he wanted to do with Snookie. But she just couldn't. Not today, and not with the pain. Plus, she was starting to feel like she was coming down with something, so that was probably making the pain worse. At least she'd have the weekend to recuperate.

"We need to talk," he said as soon as she stepped out of the car.

"Can it wait?" she asked. "To be perfectly honest, I've had a long day, and I'm not feeling well."

He looked at her with such concern and compassion that had things been different between them, she'd have wanted a hug. Well, she still did, but that would only make the pain in her heart worse.

"Give me five minutes, and then you can go rest. I'd like to talk in the tack room, where we can have some privacy."

The only reason he could possibly want privacy was if he'd had a change of heart. But from his stiff posture and firm tone, he acted almost mad at her.

She followed him into the tack room, and he closed the door behind them.

"Turn around," he said.

Nicole stared at him. "What's going on?"

"I want you to turn around and slide your shirt down so I can see the back of your right shoulder."

Nicole closed her eyes. He knew. But how? And then she remembered that she'd hidden her ruined shirt in the tack room until she could get it out without being noticed.

"It's not what you think," she said, remaining facing him.

"So then why was your bloody shirt wadded up in a corner of the tack room? And why does it have what looks like bite marks on the back of your right shoulder area?"

"I don't know." Tears ran down her face as she tried to come up with a reasonable explanation that didn't involve her showing him exactly what he was looking for.

Fernando took a step toward her. "Nicole, I promised you I'd do whatever it took for you to keep Snookie.

But I can't help you if you're not telling me everything. Why can't you trust me?"

She brushed at her eyes. "Why do you think? You're not very forthcoming, either, and you haven't done anything to show you trust me. That you trust in us. All your talk about faith—it doesn't seem to apply to you, or to us."

He looked at her like she was crazy. But she didn't feel well, and he'd broken her heart, and now, if anyone knew what had happened with Snookie, she'd lose her, too.

As the tears ran down her face, he wrapped his arms around her. "I'm sorry," he said. "You want more from me than I can give, and I've never promised you any of that. But I did promise to help with Snookie, which I can't do if you won't tell me what happened."

Fernando held her as she sobbed, and even though she knew it was crossing a lot of the boundaries they'd both tried setting, it felt so good to be held by him. Why couldn't he love her? What was so wrong with her that made men unwilling to love her? And why did she still want someone who obviously didn't feel enough of the same way to do something about it?

Taking a deep breath, Nicole pulled away, then told Fernando what had happened.

He nodded slowly, like he was processing, except it only made the angry expression on his face worse.

"You should have told me right away," he said.

She tried to glare at him, but the effort made her head hurt. "I wouldn't have been in the barn that night in the first place had you bothered to show up for dinner with Ricky. You weren't around to tell."

The fire in his gaze hurt almost as much as the pain in her shoulder. "Don't make this about that. You could have told me the next day. Or called. Or texted. The fact that Snookie bit you has an important impact on her training that I needed to know. She's been acting strange all week, and now I know why. I get that you don't want to lose her, but your stubbornness has created a huge setback in Snookie's training."

Tears filled her eyes at his harsh words. Maybe she deserved them, but it didn't feel like Fernando was on her side anymore. But at least now he knew, and maybe he could help her fix what had gone wrong.

She opened her mouth to speak, but her head hurt so much that it felt almost impossible.

"Are you okay?" Fernando asked. "You really must not be feeling well, because you look awful. I'm sorry to lay all this on you now, and I guess I should have waited since you said you wanted to go to bed."

He looked like he wanted to say more, but he was starting to get fuzzy, and her head was pounding even harder.

The next thing she knew, she was in his arms, and he was carrying her out of the barn. It felt good to have his arms around her, and to be surrounded by that familiar scent.

"Why can't you love me? Why doesn't anyone love me the way I want to be loved? Why did Snookie have to bite me? I was just hugging her and loving on her."

She was babbling now, and she probably shouldn't have said all those things. But Fernando was looking at her so tenderly, it was easy to pretend that things were different between them. Maybe when she felt better, they could talk again and find a way to make things work. Or maybe she could figure out a way to stop loving people who didn't love her back in the same way.

Fernando would have liked to have written off her feverish babbling as nonsense, but he heard the pain in her words that came from her heart. He hadn't meant for her to fall in love with him, and he hated that his desire to protect her only fed into her insecurities that she was unlovable. It was far from the truth, but how could he convince her that all his actions were based on love?

As he gathered her in his arms, he looked at her shoulder. The angry red streaks coming from the wound told him this wasn't a virus she was fighting but an infection from the horse bite that she was hiding from everyone. In trying to keep it a secret to protect Snookie, she'd endangered her life.

Walking out of the barn with Nicole in his arms, the first person he came upon was Shane. There was no way he could hide this from the other man.

Shane came running toward him. "What happened?"

"Nicole is very ill," Fernando said. "We need to get her to the emergency room right away."

"I'll get my truck," Shane said. "I'm sure Leah will want to come, so one of you can sit in the back seat with Nicole, and Erin can stay with the boys. I wonder what made her so sick. She was fine this morning at breakfast."

How was he supposed to lie to this man, who was so worried about his future sister-in-law?

"Snookie bit her, and it became infected. She kept it

hidden from all of us, because she was afraid you would take her horse away."

As he spoke, Nicole's sisters approached, worry written all over their faces.

"Do you think she'll be okay?" Erin asked. "And how do you know that's what happened?"

Fernando adjusted Nicole in his arms, knowing that he couldn't keep holding her for much longer. "Let's just get her in the truck. I can explain on the way to the hospital."

Shane pulled the truck up right next to him and helped Fernando get Nicole in the back seat. At first, he let go of her to let Leah take over, but Nicole cried out and clutched him so tightly that he couldn't bear to leave her.

"It's okay," Leah said. "She wants you, and I'd much rather her be comfortable while she's out of it."

Fernando nodded as he adjusted Nicole in his arms while Leah buckled her sister in.

As they drove, Fernando explained to Shane and Leah what he'd found in the barn and the result of his confrontation with Nicole.

"When you approached me in the barn earlier, Shane, I'd just found the bloodied shirt. I should have told you then, but I wanted to give Nicole the chance to explain first. I just never imagined that the bite had become infected. But judging from the wound, it was probably hard for her to reach to clean it."

"I just don't understand why she wouldn't have asked for our help," Leah said.

Fernando looked down at Nicole and brushed her hair off her sweaty forehead. "She didn't want to lose Snookie. Based on her incoherent mumblings, she thinks Snookie is all she has to love. Yes, she has you guys, but it's not the same. The way Brandon left her, she feels unworthy of love."

He didn't add that his seeming rejection of her probably hadn't made things any better. Given the murderous look he saw on Shane's face every time the other man glanced into the rearview mirror to check on them, he was pretty sure Shane would have words with him later. And maybe Fernando deserved it, giving Nicole hope then taking it away from her.

But Fernando would do whatever it took to at least save Snookie for Nicole. He couldn't give her what she wanted, at least in terms of their relationship, but he had to help her keep her horse.

"You said that if Snookie bit again, you'd make Nicole get rid of her. But that's exactly why we're racing her to the emergency room right now. Can't you see how desperate she is to keep her horse? Don't break Nicole's heart."

Shane was silent for a moment and then he said, "I'm not going to talk about this right now. I know you mean well, but this just proves what a danger Snookie is. These infections can be life-threatening."

"And if she hadn't been so afraid of having Snookie taken from her, she wouldn't have hidden her injury, and she would've gotten proper treatment in the first place. I'm not trying to blame you here, but I am saying that you cannot make good on your threat to take that horse from her."

"That's exactly what it sounds like to me," Shane said. "I'm doing what's best for my family. Someone has to be man enough to do the right thing, even if it's hard."

The other man's words stung, reminding him of their

earlier argument. Maybe Fernando was a coward, but Shane wasn't much better, refusing to see sense when it came to this horse.

"I'm not the only one who needs to do the right thing here," Fernando insisted.

"Enough!" Leah's voice echoed through the truck. "You two do your idiotic manly garbage on your own time. But, Shane, you need to focus on the road so that you don't kill us all before we get my sister to the hospital. And, Fernando, you can save your lectures for when he won't be too distracted to hear them. You're both being a couple of jerks right now, and the only thing we need to focus on is getting Nicole safely to the hospital for treatment."

She had a point, and Fernando felt guilty for arguing with Shane while Shane was trying to drive. "You're right, I'm sorry. I'm just worried about Nicole, and the desperation that got her to this point."

"We're all worried about Nicole," Leah said. "But blaming each other and arguing isn't going to get her any better. I agree, we will need to discuss the fact that Nicole felt it necessary to hide her injury from all of us. But let's get her well first."

The tears in Leah's voice were evident, and as Fernando looked down at Nicole again, he prayed that she would realize just how deeply she was loved—by all of them.

Chapter Twelve

Nicole woke feeling groggy, like her sleep hadn't been restful. When she lifted her arm to rub her eyes, she realized she was hooked up to an IV.

She must have really been sick. This was some virus.

As she rubbed her eyes and looked around the room, she noticed Leah was sitting beside her.

"Good. You're awake. You probably have realized that you're in the hospital. You've got a nasty infection from the horse bite you were hiding from us."

Nothing like a sister to be direct. But at least now she knew that everyone knew. Which meant there was no saving Snookie. Tears filled her eyes.

Leah took her hand. "None of that. I told Fernando and Shane that they aren't allowed to discuss it until you're well, and that if I hear any more of their idiotic manly posturing over you, I'm going to send them to bed without any supper." Leah gave a firm look to Fernando, who was standing on the other side of the room.

Then she grinned. "Okay, maybe that wasn't a very good threat. But they know I mean business, and that your well-being is what's most important here. But I did want you to know that we know the truth, so you can stop hiding things and focus on getting well."

"And Snookie?"

"I have half a mind to send her to bed without any supper, too."

The tears that had filled Nicole's eyes began to fall, and Leah gave her hand another squeeze. "Can't you understand that you and your safety are most important to us?"

Nicole shook her head. "None of you understand just how much she means to me."

"I get it," Leah said. "But you could have died."

"I didn't think I had any other choice," Nicole whispered.

Fernando came around the other side of the bed and touched her arm gently. "I would have helped you. I would have advocated for both you and Snookie if you had just told me the truth."

"Like you told me the truth about your past? You didn't tell me until you had no other choice, which is what I did."

She hadn't meant to hurt him, but the wounded look on his face made her feel bad. But that was just it. People expected things of her but weren't willing to give the same back.

"That's different," Fernando said. "But apparently, Shane knew all along. He ran a background check on me."

As Nicole tried processing Fernando's words, Leah turned, and Nicole could see Shane standing in the background.

"You ran a background check on Fernando?" Leah asked, sounding annoyed.

"I'm not going to let just anyone stay on your property, given that so many people I love live there. Besides, I run them on everyone I hire."

Leah's posture softened, but Nicole could tell that the couple would be discussing things later. Maybe her sister didn't always side with Shane just because they were engaged. Maybe she should have tried talking to Leah or Erin.

Then Leah looked over at Fernando. "What's in your past that's so scary?"

"I learned to train horses in prison," he said. "People don't respond well to hearing about my felony conviction, so I only share it when absolutely necessary. I'm sorry if that makes you uncomfortable, but I promise I'm not a danger to you or your sons."

Nicole reached up and took Fernando's hand. "None of us would believe that of you."

He nodded, like he knew she was telling the truth, but there was still a barrier between them. She remembered, from shortly before she passed out, him expressing his deep hurt at the fact that she hadn't confided in him. And maybe she should have. But she was trying so hard to keep her distance, knowing that he was unwilling to love her the way she needed to be loved.

If only it didn't hurt so much to have him hold her at arm's length.

"I agree," Leah said. "I don't have all the details, but whatever happened, you're clearly a good man now. And even though I'm not sure I agree with Shane's decision to run a background check on you, if there had been anything disturbing in that report, Shane would have told us. Still, we all have to figure out a way to trust each other and not keep so many secrets."

A fresh wave of tears trickled down Nicole's face, and Fernando brushed them away. "Please don't cry. I'm sure that if you knew then just how much everyone loves and supports you, you would have made a different decision about hiding your injury. But we can't go back. So let's find a way to move forward and make better choices."

She'd have liked to have trusted in his words, except that he wasn't living them for himself. He was making choices based on past bad experiences, and they weren't making life any better for him, or the people who loved him.

Leah squeezed Nicole's other hand. "I completely agree. I want you to know that I support you, no matter what. And it pains me to think that you couldn't trust me to help you."

Then Leah turned her gaze back to Shane. "I love you. You know that. And even though I love that you love my family as your own, you're not the boss of my family. We work together to solve our problems, and you don't get to dictate how things go all the time. Surely you can't have forgotten the lesson you learned in making decisions for me in the past. Don't do it to my sister, either."

Shane's jerky nod only made Nicole's tears flow faster. All this time, she'd been thinking that she was somehow losing her sister to him. And that their plans as a family no longer mattered. But now, she could see that Leah would still always be there for her.

Why had it taken getting so sick for Nicole to realize it?

She looked up at her sister. "I'm sorry for not trusting you. I was just worried that with as close as you and Shane are, you considered his opinion above all others. Especially since you said you fully trusted his judgment when it came to Snookie."

Leah bent and kissed her on top of her head. "You will always be my little sister, and I will always love you. No matter what, I am here for you. And you have to believe that I always have your best interests at heart. Shane is right to be concerned about Snookie's behavior. But I would never ask you to give up an animal you so desperately love and have spent your whole life waiting to have without exhausting all other options. I should have spoken up sooner, but I believe in you and in Fernando's ability to rehabilitate Snookie."

Then Leah looked across the bed at Fernando. "I still do."

Shane moved closer to the bed. "I never said I didn't. And I'll admit I might have been hasty in making that threat. But Snookie is still biting, and that behavior has to be addressed."

Leah gave Shane the glare that Nicole recognized as being the one she gave her boys when they were acting up. "We agreed not to discuss that right now."

It was actually kind of funny, watching Shane squirm under Leah's gaze. Nicole felt bad for not giving her sister enough credit for having a mind of her own. She might be in love, but Leah wasn't going to let anyone push her around.

Still, Nicole would rather have the discussion now, so at least she knew what she was coming home to.

"It's okay," Nicole said. "I need to know that we're going to resolve the situation with Snookie. Based on what happened, and what I've been reading about, I came to Snookie in an emotional state she didn't understand. I was hurting, brokenhearted over Fernando's unwillingness to even talk to Ricky. I clung to her, sobbing, and it scared her. Snookie had this weird version of me hanging from her neck, and she was frightened, so she acted out. I was wrong. I should have remembered Fernando's lessons about horses feeding off our energy, but I was so caught up in my own pain that I forgot and acted inappropriately around my horse."

As she gave voice to the conclusions that she'd come to, it only made her feel worse about the situation. Even though she now knew she could confide in her sister more, it still hurt that her best friend was a horse, and even that horse couldn't be what she needed her to be.

Fernando squeezed her hand. "I'm sorry. I didn't mean to hurt you with my decision. But can't you understand that it was just as difficult for me as it was for you? Yes, I would love to be a horse trainer. But you don't realize how many times I have tried, only to have that dream torn from me."

He turned to Shane. "You might call me a chicken, and maybe you're right. But a man can only be beaten up and broken so many times."

Nicole had no idea what Fernando was talking about, but as she saw the expressions exchanged between the two men, it was clear they'd had some harsh words over Fernando's decision. And even though it still felt like

Fernando was abandoning her by not even trying, the pain in his eyes made her realize that it had probably cost him more than she could ever know.

While it hurt that Fernando wasn't willing to take a risk for her sake, she now realized that this truly was about Fernando and his insecurities. It wasn't about her not being enough for him, but about him believing himself not enough for her. She'd done her best to convince him differently, but until he realized it for himself, nothing she said would make a difference.

Whatever Fernando's journey needed to be in the situation, it was his journey. She couldn't force that on him, nor could she take responsibility for that failure upon herself. He might say he was doing this because he loved her, but until he learned to love himself, he wasn't capable of loving her the way she needed him to.

And suddenly, the pain of losing Fernando didn't hurt so much anymore. Keeping him wasn't her responsibility. If he didn't want to stay, she had to let him go. And she had to pray that wherever the journey took him, God would keep them both safe.

The only thing that was her responsibility was herself. And, if she could convince the rest of her family of it, Snookie.

"All right, then," Nicole said, pushing the button to raise the bed higher. Fernando wasn't sure what had just happened, but whatever it was, he was looking at a different Nicole.

"What are we going to do about Snookie?" she asked.

They all looked at Shane.

"What?" he asked. "You've all made it clear that

I'm the bully who wants you to get rid of your precious horse. I'm not so unfeeling as that. I understand how much you love her. But how am I supposed to make you all understand the importance of safety? You're all new to this, and I've spent my whole life on a ranch. Why can't you trust that I have your best interests in mind?"

Then Shane turned to Leah. "You asked me to trust you, but just like we both learned in the past, that trust has to go both ways. You have to trust me, too."

Nicole had told Fernando that when they'd first gotten the ranch, Shane had bought some cows out from under them to save the sisters from making a mistake and buying a diseased herd.

Clearly, working through trust issues didn't involve overnight solutions but was a lifelong process in making a relationship work. And maybe he wasn't necessarily in a relationship, but Fernando could learn a lot from watching this couple continue to work through their problems.

Shane turned his attention back to Nicole. "You and Fernando have done a great job with Snookie so far. And I know, in you accepting responsibility for your role in getting bitten, you understand much more about horses and their behavior. But clearly you still have a lot to learn."

At least Shane sounded like he was going to give Nicole another chance with Snookie. Fernando sent up a silent prayer of thanksgiving that Nicole's mistake hadn't cost her everything.

Then Shane looked over at Fernando. "Which is why I'm counting on you to stick around to help her. You told me you would do anything so that Nicole can keep her horse. And now I'm about to see if you're a man of your word."

Somehow, Fernando knew, without Shane having even given his terms, Fernando wasn't going to like it.

"What do you want from me?" Fernando asked.

"You can't just be a weekend trainer. Snookie needs daily work, and it's clear that Nicole is not ready to take on training Snookie on her own. I know you can get Snookie to where she needs to be. The question is, are you willing to do it?"

Fernando did the mental math, trying to figure out how he could do a two-hour drive each way every day. The expectant look on Nicole's face made his heart ache. He'd made her a promise. Shane was calling him on it.

Looking down at Nicole, Fernando said, "I didn't get a chance to tell you. My uncle needs me to start work on Monday or I will lose the job. It's a two-hour drive each way."

"That's your only option," Shane said.

Fernando shook his head. "You can't be sure that Ricky would offer me the job."

"You won't even talk to him," Shane countered.

Did Shane understand exactly what he was asking of Fernando? From the challenging expression on the other man's face, it was clear that he did. And from the hopeful look in Nicole's eyes, Fernando understood why.

They all wanted him to stay. And while it felt good to have so many people behind him, they also didn't understand what it looked like when things went bad.

But he had promised Nicole that he would do whatever it took for her to keep Snookie.

He just hadn't understood that every ounce of his pride would be the cost.

Nicole had muttered something in her delirium about no one loving her the way she loved them. Loving her had already cost him so much in terms of making him face his fears. And now he'd be giving her his everything. Even though he would never be able to tell her.

Shane might be able to manipulate him into applying for a job with Ricky, but that didn't mean he was going to put Nicole's future at risk by pursuing anything with her. If Shane thought this was the ticket to Nicole's happily-ever-after, then he still had a lot to learn about what happily-ever-after looked like.

"I promised you I would do whatever it takes for you to keep Snookie, and I meant it," he said to Nicole. "So I'll talk to Ricky, apply for the job, and if I don't get it, I'll make the drive every day if necessary."

The look in her eyes was the same one she had the last time she'd tried to kiss him.

"Don't mistake this for love," he cautioned, hating himself for having to crush her hopes. It had to be enough that she could keep her horse. "I meant what I told you about us having no future. Please don't take my decision about Snookie as anything other than my keeping my promise to you."

To Shane and Leah he said, "Don't let her get her hopes up about me. I'm here for the horse, and because I made Nicole and Snookie a promise. I'll be respectful of her feelings in not leading her on, but there will be no romantic machinations from the two of you or anyone else."

Shane nodded slowly, like he realized that he'd been

caught at his own game. It felt good to know that despite all the harsh words they'd shared, Shane obviously thought enough of Fernando that he was still trying to get him and Nicole together.

But that was the thing about love.

Loving someone meant letting them go, even if it took ripping out your heart to do so.

Chapter Thirteen

Fernando shifted uncomfortably, hat in hand, as he stood in the foyer of Ricky's large ranch house. He'd known that the other man had money, given that he owned a ranch large enough to have a string of seventy-five horses and employ so many people. But looking around at the entryway leading into an expansive great room, filled with what had to have been very expensive cowboy art, he had to wonder what he'd gotten himself into.

A wiry old man entered through a set of double doors on the side of the great room.

"You must be Fernando," he said. "I'm Ricardo Ruiz IV, but everyone calls me Ricky. My family has owned the Double R Ranch since before Colorado was a state. However, I don't have anyone else to carry on the ranch. So I turned this place into a way for people to fall in love again with the cowboy lifestyle."

There was a sadness in the old man's voice, and Fernando appreciated the way he was doing his part to preserve traditions that would be lost otherwise. As Ricky continued explaining about the ranch and how it was set up, it was clear he was looking for someone who wanted to be part of the tradition as well.

Yes, Ricky wanted an employee. But he wanted someone who bought in to the ranch lifestyle just as much as Ricky did. Which wasn't a problem for Fernando. He appreciated the traditions and would love nothing better than to spend the rest of his life on a ranch, working with horses.

But it seemed almost a shame to get this old man's hopes up.

As Ricky led him out of the house and down the path to an oversize barn, Fernando's heart sank. He didn't have to enter the barn to see that the facility was a dream come true. Anyone who loved horses would love a place like this.

Fernando stopped. "Hold up a second. Before we go any further, there's something I need to tell you. I've got a record. It's been a problem for some people in the past, and I need to know now if it's going to be a problem for you."

Ricky gave him a long, hard look. "What do you take me for, a fool? I might be as old as dirt, but that doesn't mean I'm stupid. When Shane recommended you for the job, I did some digging of my own into your background. I even talked to Walt Cunningham himself. People forget I know all these folks. Walt used to ride on the rodeo circuit with my late son, Cinco, God rest his soul."

The long pause following Ricky's comment about his son made Fernando think that the old man was offering a quick prayer for his son. It was touching to see how much he still loved the boy, however old he'd been when he died. If he had been around Walt's age, he'd be somewhere in his fifties about now.

"Anyway," Ricky continued. "Walt said you're one of the finest horsemen he's ever trained. Said you were a good man who got a bum deal but made the most of it. Maybe you got something on your record, but that doesn't tell me half as much as Walt's words did. I'll want to evaluate you for myself, but I'm not going to hold the mistakes of your past against you."

That seemed to be the theme of his conversations lately about his conviction. The trouble was, people said it but their actions always proved differently. Still, it felt good to hear that Ricky had talked to Walt and Walt had said such nice things about him.

Ricky continued the tour of the barn, and it was far better than any other facility Fernando had ever seen. Working here would be a dream. Every piece of equipment Fernando could imagine wanting to try or use was available to him. And when Ricky led him out to the paddock, it only took a quick glance to know that Ricky had some of the finest horseflesh Fernando had ever encountered. None of these appeared to be the kind of project horse he was dealing with in training Snookie.

It seemed almost unfair to have such a job dangled in front of him. Naturally, Fernando would accept it if offered. It just meant it would hurt even more when the inevitable happened and Fernando was let go.

One of the wranglers brought a horse over to them. "Ricky, this is the mare I was telling you about."

Ricky gestured at Fernando. "This is Fernando, and

he's applying for the trainer job. Fernando, this is Steve. He's our head wrangler, and a fine one at that."

The mare was jumpy, tugging at the lead rope, and Steve kept giving it a jerky correction that was doing more harm than good by making the mare more anxious.

Fernando held his hand out to the palomino, whose dark golden coloring was striking. He wondered if whoever had purchased the horse had done so because she was so beautiful. "What's her name?"

"Charm," Steve said, giving the rope another jerk as the horse reared.

"She's definitely charming." Fernando smiled at him. "You don't mind if I take her for a while, do you?"

Steve handed him the rope. "Let's see what you've got."

The other man's attitude told Fernando that he felt threatened, having Fernando around. If Fernando had to guess, Steve probably wanted the job for himself, but for whatever reason, Ricky didn't want to promote him. He'd definitely need to keep his eye on Steve.

Once he had the rope, Fernando began the same basic calming exercises he'd done with Snookie. Based on what he'd seen of Steve's handling and Charm's response, the skittish horse needed more gentling, and Steve's jerky movements were scaring her.

As he had when he'd first started working with Snookie, Fernando easily fell into a rhythm where he shut out all his hopes, all his fears and any thoughts of where this job would lead, and connected with Charm.

If this test was meant to make him not want the job, they'd chosen the wrong horse. Charm needed him.

Just like Snookie needed him. And, as he found himself bonding with Charm, he knew this was what he was meant to do.

When he led Charm back to Ricky and Steve, he could see the respect on Ricky's face, and the disdain written all over Steve's. He'd been right to peg Steve as being jealous, and he hoped it wouldn't be a problem as Ricky held his hand out to Fernando.

"That is some of the finest horsemanship I've seen," Ricky said, shaking Fernando's hand. "We've still got to go over particulars, but I'm just going to tell you right now that the job is yours if you want it."

Ricky turned to Steve. "You're going to learn a lot from this man. Who knows, maybe one day, you can start training some horses, too."

Steve's expression darkened. He obviously didn't appreciate the idea of being taught more skills. Fernando knew the type. They thought they knew it all when it came to the horses, and no one could tell them otherwise.

As Fernando handed Charm back to Steve and followed Ricky out of the barn, he could feel Steve's eyes on him, probably plotting the most efficient way to get rid of him.

But that was nothing new. Fortunately for Steve, as soon as he learned about Fernando's background, he'd find plenty of ways to get rid of Fernando. At least it was a good warning that Fernando shouldn't get too attached to the job.

Everyone else might have hope that people would see him for more than what his record said he was. In the end, it was a stigma he couldn't overcome.

Still, when Ricky officially offered him the position as his head trainer, Fernando accepted.

He just hoped he didn't end up regretting it.

Since getting out of the hospital, Nicole found herself staring at the apartment over the barn more and more. Though Fernando had made it clear he had no interest in pursuing anything romantic with her, she couldn't help thinking how romantic it was that he'd gone out of his comfort zone to apply for Ricky's job so he could save her horse.

"I'm sure he'll be back soon," Leah said, coming up behind her. "We're all anxious to hear how the interview went."

Nicole turned to her sister. "I just hope it wasn't a mistake on Shane's part, making that a condition of my keeping Snookie. Maybe I should just give her up."

"Is that what you want?"

It had hurt just to say the words the first time. Nicole shook her head. "Of course not. I just hate knowing how much trouble having Snookie has caused."

She pointed at her bandaged shoulder. "This could have been the boys. Am I being selfish in fighting for her?"

Leah wrapped her arms around Nicole. "You were always one to fight for the underdog. It's one of the things I love about you. I'm not worried about having Snookie here. The boys know to stay away, and I have faith that you'll figure out what Snookie needs and be able to give that to her. Everything will be all right. It will just take time."

Everyone had been telling Nicole she was in too

much of a rush for things. And maybe she did need to learn to be more patient. Wasn't that the whole point of the training lessons with Snookie? It just seemed like she'd been waiting her whole life to get her dreams, and now that they were within reach, she didn't want to wait any longer.

Fernando's truck pulled up in front of the barn, and Nicole turned to go out to greet him.

"Give him space," Leah said. "If he didn't love you, he wouldn't have made such a sacrifice. But he's got to figure things out on his own."

Right. Because she'd pushed too hard with Brandon. Not that any of them had recognized it at the time, but at least now, she knew better.

Still, she was pleased to see that when she got outside, Fernando was headed her way.

"How'd it go?" she asked.

His smile warmed her. "Great. I'm going to enjoy working there. I'm impressed with all that Ricky offers his employees. In fact, as part of the job, there's a cabin for me to stay in. They need me on-site in case anything goes wrong with the horses."

It shouldn't hurt so much to hear that Fernando wouldn't be living over their barn anymore. Erin had said that Ricky had offered her a place to stay as well, though she hadn't taken it. Nicole supposed the arrangement was for the best and would make it easier not seeing Fernando all the time.

"Hey," he said. "I'll still come over every day to work with you and Snookie. I made it clear to Ricky that it was an important priority, and he agreed. But it will be easier for me, staying there."

Easier, how? So she wouldn't tempt him to think that maybe they had a future together? At least, unlike Brandon, Fernando was honest with her about his feelings. Still, it was hard, knowing that Fernando supposedly cared about her yet had the strangest way of showing it.

"It sounds perfect," she said. "You're going to do a great job."

He gave a nonchalant shrug. "We'll see. I don't want anyone to get their hopes up. Things like this have a way of not working out for me."

She hated how pessimistic he was about his situation and future. But this was something else he needed to figure out on his own. Fernando might have been willing to take one risk for her, but it was clear that was as far as he was willing to go.

"Have a little faith," she said instead. "It amazes me how much faith you have in God, but so little in yourself. God chose to redeem you. He's brought you this far, and just as you keep telling me to have faith in this journey, maybe you need to take your own advice. If you believe in all these good things from God for others, maybe it's time to believe the same for yourself."

Fernando looked like he wanted to argue, but then he nodded. "Maybe you're right."

She couldn't help smiling at his response, but then he shook his head.

"Don't think this means anything. It's obvious you want to help me, but there are some things that can't be fixed. I know you think I'm rejecting you, and trust me, were my situation different, I would want nothing more than to be with you. But sometimes you have to accept reality."

Nicole squared her shoulders. "People said the same thing about Snookie."

Fernando made an exasperated noise. "Snookie is different. She's an animal, and I'm talking about society."

"You don't think God is big enough to handle society?"

"God is big enough to handle anything," Fernando said.

"Except your problems."

The exasperated look on his face was almost a win. And maybe she was wrong to argue with him, especially considering the fact that pushing on this issue, or any other, was about her and her needs. What she really needed was a man who would love her enough to break through his insecurities on his own.

The realization hit her with more force than their kiss she couldn't get out of her mind. Yes, a part of her desperately wanted to be with him, but she didn't want it to be about a fight. His decision to care for her couldn't be something she'd forced, but something he joyfully gave.

That's why his sacrifice with Snookie didn't mean as much as it could have. Yes, it felt good to know that he'd sacrificed some of his pride to save her horse. But it would've felt better to her if Shane hadn't forced his hand.

Time to move on and let Fernando be who he needed to be and focus on the only thing she could control.

"Well, let's go work with Snookie, then." She looked him in the eye, gesturing to the barn. "You're right in that we have said all we need to say about personal matters. I'm not going to push you anymore. You made your feelings clear, and I respect you enough to respect your feelings. I don't agree with them, and I think you're being a hypocrite in terms of your faith. But that's for you to work out with God. And if you can look God in the eye and feel good about yourself, then more power to you. It's no longer my concern. But what is my concern is my horse. And what we're going to do about her."

For a brief moment, shock registered on Fernando's face. But then he nodded slowly. "Good. I know you're trying to help me, and it means a lot. But I can't be the man you want me to be, and you deserve better than that."

Nicole took a deep breath, allowing more confidence to fill her. "You're right. I do. I owe you a debt of gratitude for a lot of things, and even though I am hurt over how things transpired between us romantically, I'm grateful. I've settled for too little when it comes to relationships. Maybe that's why things didn't work out with Brandon. I thought that my doing everything I could to hold it together would be enough. But I want a man who is willing to work as hard as I am and hold as tightly to me as I am to him. You're not that man. And I pray that someday, God will bring him to me."

He didn't say anything as he turned and started walking toward the barn. Maybe it hadn't been fair, rubbing it in that she would find someone else. But as she spoke the words, she felt a lot of peace about letting Fernando go.

Snookie greeted her with a whinny as Nicole entered the area near her stall.

"Hey, girl," Nicole said. "I'm sorry I haven't been to see you in a couple of days. I've been sick, and I know you don't understand that. But I'm sorry for scaring you the other day."

The horse obviously had no idea what she was saying, but it felt good to say it.

Fernando handed her the halter and lead rope. Nicole entered the stall and put the halter on Snookie. As she did so, she practiced one of the things she'd learned from Fernando. She prayed. Whatever had gone wrong between her and Snookie before, she prayed that God would help her figure it out and make things right.

Nicole led Snookie into the round pen, and even though Fernando hadn't yet given her any instructions, Nicole began with the basic gentling exercises she'd done when she and Fernando had first gotten Snookie to join up with her. This time Fernando didn't enter the round pen. Instead, he stood outside the fence, watching.

And as Nicole went through the exercises she remembered, she quickly forgot all thoughts of Fernando, until she was focused solely on the horse.

She wasn't sure how long she'd been out there with Snookie, because time seemed to stand still and she and Snookie fell into the same easy rhythm they'd once had.

Once Snookie joined up with her, it felt like they had reached a deeper level than ever before.

"I love you, Snookie," she said, gently resting her head against the horse. "I'm so sorry for everything."

Snookie gave her a loving nudge, like she understood her words and was returning the apology.

Then the moment passed, and Nicole looked up. Fernando gave her a small nod, acknowledging that she'd done the right thing. Nicole led Snookie to the gate, and

Fernando let her out. As they walked to the barn in silence, things felt different between her and Fernando. Like she truly had let go of her attachment to having a future with him. Yes, she would need his help training Snookie. But they could work together as professionals, and any secret dream she had of kissing him again was hers alone.

"You did good," Fernando said. "That's exactly what I would have done. Your instincts with her are spot-on. If you remember to follow them and be patient on the other things you want from her, she'll get there eventually. Snookie clearly trusts you, and you both have a good bond."

His words of praise made her feel good. Even though Shane had made it clear that Fernando would have to be present when Nicole trained Snookie for the time being, maybe, given the fact that Nicole now understood the importance of not forcing her timing, things would go smoothly enough that Fernando's help wouldn't be needed much longer.

It was hard, letting go of the idea of having Fernando around, but Nicole was done trying to force her agenda on others. She had to trust in God's timing—even if it meant not getting what she wanted. She had to believe that whatever God had in mind, it was for the best.

Though she had to admit, she couldn't imagine having anyone better than Fernando.

Chapter Fourteen

Fernando entered the barn, checking to make sure everything was secure for the night. He'd been at the Double R for a month now, and it was crazy to think how well he'd settled in. Even though he still wasn't sure how long it would last, he could almost believe that he might have found a permanent situation. If not, he wasn't sure what he was going to do. His uncle hadn't been pleased that he'd changed his mind about the job.

But Fernando was starting to feel comfortable enough that he'd called Bob from church and asked to join one of the men's groups. Bob had even assured him that his record wasn't an issue for anyone there. Fernando wasn't fully committing to anything, but the longer things continued going well, the more he could hope he'd finally found a home.

Fernando paused at one of the stalls. Roscoe clearly hadn't eaten yet and was starting to throw a fit because of it. It had been Steve's turn to feed, but Steve's truck hadn't been in its usual spot when Fernando came to the barn.

Regardless of whose turn it was to feed the horses, they still needed to eat. He'd have words with Steve about it in the morning. Fernando went into the grain room to prepare the mixture of grain for the horses. The horses in the barn had a special diet, and Ricky was particular about making sure that they were fed properly and on time.

While the grain was soaking, he went over to the hay to begin divvying it out to the animals that got hay. However, when he grabbed the bale, he realized he didn't have a knife on him. When he turned to go back to the grain room to find one, he ran into Ricky.

"How's it going?" Ricky asked. "I thought I'd check to see how you're settling in."

Fernando shrugged. "Good. I was just getting the animals their feed."

Ricky glanced at his watch, and Fernando knew what he was thinking. It was late, and the horses should have been fed by now.

"I thought Steve would have done that already," Ricky said.

Steve already clearly resented Fernando, and it didn't seem fair to throw him under the bus, especially since it would only make the other man's attitude worse.

Fernando shrugged. "Maybe we had a misunderstanding. But I'm here now, and as soon as I head into the other room and grab a knife, I'll get it taken care of."

Ricky nodded slowly but didn't look pleased. "Isn't there a schedule on the board?"

Fernando should have realized that Ricky had his finger on the pulse of everything that happened here at Double R Ranch. Each of the wranglers rotated who was in charge of feeding on a particular day so that they all knew who was responsible for what and when. Technically, it wasn't Fernando's job to feed, and obviously, Ricky knew that.

"I'm sure it is," Fernando said. "But I'm not sure where Steve's at, and someone's got to do it."

He started toward the feed room to get a knife, but Ricky reached into his pocket. "Here. You can use my knife. I'm surprised you don't carry one yourself."

Fernando shrugged. "I usually do, but I was using it earlier in my truck, and I accidentally left it there."

He took the knife and cut the string on the hay. But as he handed the knife back to Ricky, he took a closer look. "This is a nice knife."

The pocketknife was good quality, old and worn, clearly Ricky's favorite tool. The wooden handle was inlaid with silver and turquoise with the Double R Ranch brand.

As Ricky took the knife, he grinned. "That knife has been in our family for as long as the ranch, passed down from father to son. I use it every day, and it reminds me of the responsibility to our family's tradition."

"It's gorgeous," Fernando said. "You're very blessed to have such a wonderful treasure from your father. Mine died when I was young, and it was just my mom, raising my sister and me."

"That must have been hard," Ricky said.

"My mother did the best she could, given the circumstances. She's a good woman, and even though things were strained between us for a while because of my conviction, I think we're finding our way. It's hard for her, having sacrificed so much, trying to keep my sister and me on a good path. I went to prison, and now my sister is dead. I know she thinks she's a failure, but it wasn't because of her choices, but ours."

He wasn't sure why he was saying all of this about his upbringing, since he usually didn't talk about it, but something about Ricky made him think of the father he'd wished he'd had. By all accounts, his late father had been a good man, and he'd like to think he'd have been something like Ricky.

Ricky nodded slowly. "It's hard for a parent not to blame themselves. After that Lane Frost fellow died in that famous bull riding accident, I told Cinco he shouldn't ride the bulls. But the more I told him not to do it, the more he wanted to. I just wanted to keep him safe. Sometimes I wonder if I could have done things differently, but his wife, Luanne, told me nothing would have kept him from riding, because of how much he loved it."

The grief in the old man's voice was evident, and Fernando gave him a comforting smile. "It sounds like you've at least got her. Did they have any children?"

Ricky shook his head sadly. "We haven't spoken since Cinco died. She didn't want to continue dwelling in the sadness, so she moved on with her new life. Last I heard, she'd married and was living somewhere in Texas."

"Was Cinco your only child?"

Ricky nodded slowly. "Rosie had a tough time getting pregnant and having Cinco was too hard on her body, so we agreed not to have more children. It never occurred to me that there wouldn't be anyone left to carry on the Double R after I'm gone."

The man sounded so morose that Fernando couldn't help patting him on the shoulder lightly. "Hopefully you've still got a few more good years in you."

Ricky shrugged. "Maybe. No one really knows how long we have. Who would've thought that I would outlive my son by thirty years?"

Then Ricky grinned. "But if you're worried about your job, don't. I put the ranch under a trust, with the idea of preserving it for future generations to understand ranching. Erin is helping work out the details with my lawyer."

Nicole's sister was smart, and Fernando had no doubt that the Double R was in good hands with her.

"Thanks for sharing with me," Fernando said. "I don't plan on having a family of my own, so it's a real privilege to be part of something like this that's preserving a family tradition."

Ricky gave him a funny look. "What about Erin's sister? Everyone says you're sweet on Nicole."

Fernando let out a long sigh. He should have expected this, considering everyone else seemed to be pushing him toward Nicole whether he liked it or not. He was grateful that at least she was respecting his wishes.

"Unfortunately," Fernando said, "that isn't going to go anywhere. She deserves more than I can give her, and we've both come to a place of accepting that."

Ricky snorted. "What exactly does she need you to give her? The Taj Mahal? All a woman really needs is the love of a good man. She'll have that with you. It's easy for us to think that we owe our loved ones something more. I think about all of the things that I wish

I could've done with Cinco and Rosie, and it's always about the time I could've spent with them and the love I could've given them."

A sad look crossed Ricky's face. "The truth is, Cinco and I had stopped talking about a year before he died. His mother had just died, and I was pressuring him to come back to the ranch. He just wanted to ride the bulls. He told me that if I really loved him, I'd come out and watch. But I never once saw my son riding a bull. Sure, I saw pictures. But it's not the same."

The regret in the older man's voice was evident, and though Fernando appreciated the advice to spend time with your children, he wouldn't be having any to spend time with.

Ricky shook his head slowly. "If you love Nicole, don't feed yourself any of that garbage about needing things to be perfect to make your relationship work. What you really need is love. I didn't understand that with Cinco.

"I've never told anyone this," Ricky said. "But when Cinco died, Luanne was pregnant. She told me the best way I could honor his memory would be to leave her and the baby alone. My biggest regret in life was that I never tried harder to have a relationship with them."

Though Fernando appreciated the old man sharing his wisdom, he wasn't sure how any of it applied to him. Fernando was deliberately making choices that would prevent him from having anyone to drive away.

"I figured I already messed up my own son's life," Ricky continued. "So maybe the best thing would be to let Luanne take her child and do a better job."

A sad look crossed the old man's face, and Fernando wondered what it was like to live with such deep regret.

"People used to ask me why I hadn't remarried after Rosie died. I was young. Some might have even called me good-looking. And with a ranch like mine, I don't think it's a brag to say I was a catch. But I'd messed things up so badly the first time, I didn't want to ruin anyone else's life. People thought that I'd been too in love with Rosie after she died to remarry. But the truth is, I knew what a lousy husband and father I'd been the first time, and I didn't want to hurt anyone else."

Then Ricky grinned. "I like to flirt, but I've never led any woman to believe I'm available for anything else. Sometimes I think I should have thrown my hat in the ring again just in case there was someone willing to take a chance on an old fool like me. And now it's too late."

He looked Fernando up and down. "I never told anyone any of this. It's none of their business. But I hate to see you waste your life on being alone, because it's a lonely life. You have a good woman willing to love you, if you'll only let her.

"Sometimes I dream about Rosie, about Cinco and about that baby I never did get the chance to know. I didn't fight for any of them. If you care about Nicole, then fight for her. Maybe you can't give her the life you think she deserves, but maybe that's not the life she wants. At least give it a shot. My grandchild is grown now. I don't even know if it was a boy or girl. I tried looking for Luanne once, but I never did find her. Like I said, she remarried and moved away. I assume the kid has that guy's name."

Ricky shook his head slowly, tears in his eyes. "Who

would have thought that the Double R as a family tradition would end, not because there wasn't another Ruiz to take over, but because the last one was too much of a fool to go after him."

"It doesn't have to be that way," Fernando said. "You could always look for the child now. With the advances in technology, it's easier to find people. You regret not taking that chance then, so why not now?"

Ricky gave him a look that cut him to the core. "Are you in any position to talk to me about taking risks? I know Shane had to blackmail you into applying for this job. Son, that's not a way to live your life. I can't tell you what to do, and I'm sure not going to let you tell me what to do. But if you had any brains at all, you'd figure out what you wanted in life, and even if you had a snowball's chance in Death Valley of getting it, you'd do whatever it took to get there. I've had a good life, but none of it matters because I don't have love."

Fernando would have to admit that it was a lonely life. And he pictured his life, if he lived to be as old as Ricky, and what it would look like, being so alone. Sure, Ricky had a lot of friends, and people in the community respected him. But Fernando wasn't so naive as to think that it replaced those deep personal connections of having a family.

Still, how could he risk putting Nicole through the ups and downs that his record inevitably led to? He could handle the life he had left to live, knowing that he'd protected the woman he loved from getting hurt.

He looked over at Ricky. "How old are you, anyway?"

Ricky chuckled. "Eighty-three years young, and

don't you forget it. I'm a lot smarter than you whipper-snappers, so don't think you can pull one over on me."

"I wasn't going to try." Fernando grinned, knowing that Ricky's warning had nothing to do with Fernando's record.

"We'll see about that," Ricky said, turning to leave the barn. "You'd be surprised at the shenanigans people think they can get away with."

He paused at the door and looked back at Fernando. "Just remember that you can lie to yourself all you want, but don't give up on a good woman like Nicole because of those lies. None of us believe them, so maybe you should start taking a hard look at the truth."

The truth.

The truth was, Fernando wasn't as happy as he liked to tell people. Some nights, he lay awake in bed, thinking of the kiss he and Nicole had shared. He'd liked the feeling of having Nicole in his arms, and seeing the look of love in Nicole's eyes.

But what happened when something bad happened, and the convicted felon got the blame? What if he couldn't keep a job and provide for her?

Everyone kept telling him to take a risk, but no one understood just what Fernando was risking.

He finished feeding the horses, and as he was leaving the barn, he noticed Steve's truck parked nearby. Fernando felt the hood and noted that it was cool. Which meant Steve had been back long enough to realize that Fernando was doing the feeding for him. At some point, Fernando was going to have to have words with Steve, but he'd save it for later. He was tired, and his heart hurt.

Tonight he was going to his lonely cabin when the

woman he loved would be sitting at home, thinking he didn't love her, and there wasn't a thing he could do about it.

Nicole knew she was being an idiot, but when Erin invited the family out to a barbecue at Ricky's, she couldn't bring herself to go. Yes, the entire community was invited, and usually Nicole liked going to the Double R. But even though she and Fernando had found a way to work together without all their stuff coming up between them, she wasn't sure she could find a way to leave it alone hanging out on a social level.

As much as she would have liked to have said she was over him, in the past month since Fernando had gone to work for Ricky, part of her was still as in love with him as ever. She'd never felt like this after Brandon's death. The deep longing. The ache.

Her phone beeped with a text. Erin had forgotten the dressing for the salad their family was bringing and needed Nicole to run it over.

Probably a deliberate ploy to get her there, but maybe Nicole would arrive, Fernando would be flirting with a pretty girl and she'd be able to say that he was a pig and move on.

Not likely, since that wasn't the kind of man Fernando was, but she could hope. Anything to get her heart to stop hurting. At least Janie and some of the other women from the Bible study would be there. She'd been joining them the past few Sundays for lunch after church, and even though she wouldn't say she'd found new besties, she was happy with how her friendships were growing.

When Nicole arrived at Ricky's, the barbecue was in full swing.

"Nicole!" Ricky gave her a big hug. "Have you thought about going out with me yet?"

She knew he was teasing, since he said that to her every time. But then he nudged her. "Okay, since you won't date me, why don't you go put Fernando out of his misery? I don't know why you two are being such fools, but you'd better hurry up and marry him while you're still young enough to enjoy it."

Nicole shook her head. "It takes two to make a relationship work. And the other party has made it clear that's not happening. I'm not chasing after someone who isn't going to give me his all. I'm worth more than that."

Ricky grinned. "Are you sure you don't want to marry me instead? I'm quite the catch, and I need a strong woman like you to keep me in line."

"There's no keeping you in line," Nicole said, laughing. "And if you really love someone, you don't want to keep them in line. Instead, you want to love and support them in being fully who they are."

Ricky burst out laughing, but before he could answer, a man came up to him and whispered something in his ear.

Immediately, the laughter turned to a look of deep concern. "Are you sure?"

The other man nodded.

"Let's go talk to him," Ricky said. Then he turned to Nicole. "You'll have to excuse me for a minute. I've got some business to take care of."

As Nicole nodded, Ricky turned and walked across

the area where the barbecue was set up. She watched as he and the other man approached Fernando.

What was going on?

None of her business, and yet, as she watched the exchange between the three men, she couldn't help wanting to go over and defend Fernando. Whatever was going on, he was obviously in trouble.

She started walking in that direction, and Shane stepped in front of her.

"Hey, Nicole. Glad you changed your mind about coming. We've got a spot over here, if you want to join us."

"That's okay, thanks. I think Fernando is in some kind of trouble." She gestured to where he was standing, talking with Ricky and the other man.

"That's Jesse, the ranch foreman. And you're right. He doesn't look happy. I wonder what's going on."

Nicole only half listened as she brushed past Shane to find out, but Shane grabbed her arm.

"He won't like it if you interfere. In fact, I really need to talk to you both about my interference, but I'd hoped to do it with both of you present. Let's wait until they finish their discussion, and we can all talk."

She shrugged off his grasp and continued on her way.

"I didn't do it," Fernando was saying as Nicole arrived.

"I'm willing to hear your explanation," Ricky said. "I just want to know how my missing knife ended up in your cabin."

Nicole took a deep breath. The expression on Fernando's face was heartbreaking. She didn't need to hear his answer to believe there had to be some mistake. Fernando wouldn't have taken it.

Footsteps behind her told her that Shane had followed her. Probably to keep her from saying or doing anything stupid. But at least he could also be a witness to Fernando's character and that he'd never take anything from someone else, least of all Ricky.

Maybe Fernando couldn't love her the way she wanted, but that didn't mean she could turn off the way she cared about him. She could tell by the way he looked at her that he'd rather her go away and not witness whatever was going down.

But she gave him a firm look to let him know that no matter what, she was here to stay.

Chapter Fifteen

Fernando should have known something like this was coming. Other than dealing with Steve's attitude, things here had been going well. Too well. Like he'd finally found a place where he could be comfortable and breathe easily.

Before he could answer Ricky, he saw Nicole and Shane arrive. Even though it killed him to have her witness his humiliation, at least now she'd understand why having a future together would be impossible. Whenever things went missing anywhere near Fernando, he'd always be blamed.

Fernando squared his shoulders and looked at Ricky. "I didn't take your knife. I have no idea how it got in my cabin. But I didn't put it there."

Ricky looked him up and down, then over at Jesse. "How'd you find it in Fernando's cabin?"

"I was looking for Fernando, and the door was open. I saw the knife on the counter, so I came to talk to you, since I knew it was missing and you were asking folks if they'd seen it."

Jesse turned to Fernando. "I'm not necessarily accusing you of stealing. Just wondering how it came to be there."

Oh, he was accusing. Fernando knew the look. Even though he and Jesse got along fine, as far as Fernando knew, he also knew that sometimes the people he thought he could trust were the ones who stabbed him in the back first chance they got.

"Of course Fernando wouldn't steal it," Nicole said. "I'm sure there's a reasonable explanation for how the knife got in his cabin."

Fernando turned to look at her. Why did she have to involve herself? He hadn't asked for her help, and the last thing he wanted was for her to alienate her friends by sticking up for him.

"What is it?" Ricky asked.

Steve joined them, looking gleeful that there was trouble and Fernando was in the middle of it.

"I have no idea how your knife got into my cabin," Fernando repeated. "I'm sorry. I have no explanation."

"Wasn't he admiring your knife the other day?" Steve asked.

How did Steve know that? Fernando examined the other man's face. Yes, Fernando had admired the knife. He and Ricky had shared a great conversation over it. But that didn't mean Fernando would steal it.

Ricky looked thoughtful, then pulled the knife out of his pocket. "He was."

Turning the knife over in his hands, Ricky seemed to be thinking back to that evening. Was he trying to remember if there'd been a greedy look in Fernando's eyes?

"If I was going to steal something," Fernando said,

"why would I steal something so obvious? That knife has been in your family for generations, and I'm sure everyone knows it's yours. If anyone found me with it, people would know I'd stolen it. Do you really think I'm that stupid?"

"Of course you're not," Nicole said. "Plus, you'd never steal."

He brought his attention back to her. "I can tell you're trying to help, but please don't. I know how this is going to go. We'll talk about it for a while, but because the knife was found in my cabin and no one can explain how it got there, I'll be asked to leave."

Fernando exhaled sharply. "This is why I didn't want to do this. I'm just glad it happened before I got too attached, because it's how things inevitably work out."

Then he turned to Ricky. "I didn't steal your knife. I know how much it means to you, and our conversation meant a lot to me. I'd never do something like that to someone who's done so much for me."

Fernando took a deep breath. "I'll go pack my things."

As he turned to leave, Nicole stepped in front of him. "No, you won't. Number one, you didn't take the knife. Number two, no one can prove that you did. And if they want to try, then they need to get the sheriff in here to treat it like a real crime."

He closed his eyes and said a brief prayer. He loved that she believed in him, but she didn't understand the difficulty in getting a fair hearing with his record.

"I appreciate what you're trying to do," he said. "But you need to understand that even if I fight this time, there's going to be a next time. And a next time."

She squared up against him, her small frame a contrast to his own. Her expression was that of a fierce warrior, and oh, how he wished he had that same fight in him.

"Or maybe if you stood up for yourself, people would know they can't railroad you. Maybe your real crime is that you're not willing to stand up for yourself."

The fury in her eyes wasn't about him being falsely accused, he could see that. And suddenly, he had to wonder if maybe she was right.

Did he want to leave the Double R?

No.

Did he want a life without Nicole?

Absolutely not.

And as he thought about his conversation with Ricky and all the old man's regrets, he realized that in some ways, the two men were the same. Ricky hadn't fought for the ones he loved or been willing to risk making another mistake.

How was Fernando any different?

Fernando turned to Ricky. "Nicole is right. I'm not going to give up without a fight this time. I'm not sure how the knife got on my counter. My cabin, like many of the other cabins on the property, was unlocked. Who's to say that Jesse or someone else didn't put it there?"

Then he remembered what Steve had said about him admiring it. "And how does Steve know that I admired it? I was in the barn, doing his chores, because he hadn't shown up to do them himself. Was he listening in on our conversation rather than doing his work?"

As he spoke, he could see the wheels turning in Ricky's head. Ricky nodded. "You do have a point. It is an interesting coincidence that my knife went missing right after we talked about it in what should have been a private conversation, and it was found in your cabin."

Then Ricky turned toward Steve. "And I am interested to hear why you hadn't fed the horses on time even though you were on the schedule to do so. It does seem mighty suspicious, especially since you've consistently been complaining about Fernando and saying you don't think he's right for the job."

Ricky pulled the knife out of his pocket again. "If we fingerprinted my knife, I know we'd find Fernando's prints on it, because I let him use it. But would we find yours, Steve? You've never had my permission to use my knife."

Steve didn't respond.

Then Erin stepped forward. "With the trail cams you've installed on the property, while there isn't one we've had specifically trained on Fernando's cabin, I think there's one with enough of a view that we could easily see if Steve entered the cabin at any point."

Fernando hadn't seen Erin join them, but as he looked around, he realized that quite a crowd had gathered. People always wanted to witness the drama. But for the first time, Fernando wasn't as fearful of everyone running him off the way he'd always figured they would.

No one had ever been on his side like this before.

Erin turned to Fernando. "Has Steve ever had permission to be in your cabin?"

"No," Fernando said. "I've never given him permission to be in my cabin, and he's never come by, to my knowledge."

Ricky looked at Steve. "Is there anything you want

to tell us? If not, we'll go watch the trail cam footage to see who's been in and out of Fernando's cabin. If there's any reason to believe someone was there without his permission, we'll be looking into whether that person could have had anything to do with my knife being in Fernando's cabin."

Even though Fernando knew Ricky to be a fair man, and even though Ricky had already given some indication of not believing Fernando had taken his knife, it finally hit him. Ricky didn't think Fernando had done it. And even before the crowd had gathered, Ricky hadn't accused Fernando of taking the knife. He'd simply asked what Fernando knew about it, and if Fernando knew how it had gotten into his cabin.

Maybe Ricky had never believed Fernando had taken it at all.

"I could have done like Jesse did, just gone in to see if Fernando was there. Maybe I had something to talk to Fernando about," Steve said.

"Like what?" Fernando asked.

Suddenly, all these years of taking the fall for things he hadn't done weighed upon him. He'd thought it was easier not fighting back because he'd never thought anyone would believe him. Especially since it hadn't mattered with his court case, even though the DA knew he was innocent. People had their own agendas and wanted to use Fernando to accomplish their ends.

But what about Fernando's ends?

His dreams? His goals? The woman he loved standing beside him, who'd practically begged him to fight for her?

He'd been willing to walk away from it all.

Not anymore.

Steve still hadn't answered, but Fernando didn't need him to.

"I get it," Fernando said. "You wanted my job. I'm sure it must be disappointing to want something and not get it, but setting someone else up for a fall isn't the way to do it. I'd have worked with you, helped you. And, just as Ricky had suggested, I would have taught you how to train horses so that you'd be able to move up, maybe into a position like mine someday."

Steve only looked angrier at Fernando's words. But that wasn't Fernando's problem. He'd done everything he could to do the right thing, and he wasn't responsible for how Steve responded. What was Fernando's responsibility was doing the right thing for himself, and for the people he loved.

Fernando looked at the gathered crowd. He figured word about his past had already gotten out, but it was time for him to own it and let the chips fall where they may. The people he cared about already knew and accepted him for it, so maybe it was time to stop fearing the rest of the community finding out as well.

"I can see why someone would want to make it look like I'd stolen Ricky's knife. In case any of you didn't know, I spent some time in prison. I was convicted of being an accomplice to a robbery in which a woman was killed. I had nothing to do with the crime, but I was too scared to speak up and tell the truth about what I knew. For that, I am guilty. And even though I lost a lot of my life because of that mistake, I don't regret my time in prison. There, I learned to work with mustangs, and I learned to bond with the horse. I gained confidence in everything but myself."

As he spoke, he could feel a weight lifting off him. "However, I'm done paying for my crime of silence. I keep committing that crime, fearing how people will treat me because of my record. But according to the law, I've paid my debt to society. And according to God, I've been forgiven. I just haven't been willing to accept it. Maybe that means some of you folks don't trust me. But I hope, in time, just like these good people have, you'll learn the kind of man I am."

Fernando looked over at Nicole, who had tears in her eyes. He held his hand out to her. "And I hope you can forgive me for pushing you away. I thought I was acting out of love for you, but really, it was out of fear for myself. I can't promise an easy life, but I can promise that whatever life throws at us, we'll handle it together."

Nicole came forward and wrapped her arms around him. "That's all I've ever wanted from you."

As he held her tight, he never wanted to let go. He kissed her gently as he whispered, "I love you."

She gave him a soft kiss back, then said, "I love you, too."

Her words brought tears to his eyes, and as she kissed him again, he couldn't imagine why he'd been so crazy as to fight this for so long. Applause rang out among the crowd, and he broke off the kiss, keeping Nicole close to him.

"We'll save the rest of this discussion for later, when we can be private," Fernando told her softly.

"Oh no, you won't," Shane said, stepping forward.

"If you're going to kiss Nicole like that, you'd better be putting a ring on her finger first."

Fernando kissed the top of Nicole's head. "In time."

He'd have loved to have done so right then, but it wasn't like he was rolling in cash. He'd barely gotten a decent job, and even though it came with a nice enough cabin, there was no way he'd be able to buy her a ring anytime soon.

But as he looked at Nicole, who'd had a huge diamond when she'd been engaged to Brandon, he knew that wasn't what she wanted. He remembered Adriana rolling her eyes because Nicole hadn't been comfortable with such a big ring and Adriana would have killed for one.

Fernando took a deep breath as he gazed on the woman he loved. "The truth is, I can't afford a ring. But I know that isn't the kind of thing that matters to you, so rather than holding off on the proposal until I can afford one, if you'll agree to marry me, I promise we'll find a way to work it out."

"I just want you," Nicole said, pulling him in for another kiss. "Yes, I'll marry you. And I don't want any of those things I thought I had to have in the past. No big fancy wedding, no stress, just you, me, the people we love, and if the ring has to come from a gumball machine, it's good enough for me."

As he kissed her, he thanked God for the beautiful woman in his arms. Yes, she was the most gorgeous woman he'd ever seen, but mostly that was because she had the biggest heart of anyone he'd ever known.

When she finally let go of him, she stared up at him

and smiled. "But if you gave me a horse instead of a ring, that would make both me and Snookie happy."

Then she looked over at Shane and Leah, who were holding hands with eyes full of love, and grinned. "Shane did give Leah a whole herd of cows for their engagement. I don't need an entire herd, but I do think we need at least one more horse so we can go riding together."

Fernando hugged her close. "I think I can manage that."

Then Ricky stepped forward. "As for the ring," he said, "you come on up to the house. I don't have anyone to pass stuff on to, so you come and pick something out from Rosie's jewelry box. I've hung on to it all, and it's not doing anyone any good. I think she'd be happy to know that her things are being put to good use."

There was a slight catch in his voice as he looked at Fernando. "I always wished I could have talked with Cinco the way we did that night in the barn. I wasn't sure if you'd take my advice or not, but you'll never know what it means to me that you did."

Then Ricky hesitated. "Just so you know, I never thought you took my knife. I figured there was a reasonable explanation for it, and I wanted to hear you out. I'm sorry if you thought I was accusing you."

Fernando moved out of his embrace with Nicole and held out his hand to Ricky. "I realize that now. Thanks for pushing me to face my fears rather than run from them. Maybe, since I've taken your advice, you might think about taking mine."

"Maybe I will," Ricky said slowly, taking Fernando's hand, then pulling him into a bear hug. "Thank you."

After their hug, Ricky looked over at Nicole. "And I meant what I said about that ring. Fernando did a service for me that I can never repay, and while it's none of anyone else's business, I will say that I will never forget the kind of man he is."

Then Ricky turned his attention to the crowd. "So if any of you have a problem with a good man who spent some time in prison, learning to be a better man and an even better horse trainer, you'd just as well get off my property and never come back."

He glanced over at Steve. "Including you. I'll leave it up to Fernando whether you stay or go, but this is your only warning that I won't tolerate any more shenanigans. You should fess up and apologize if you did it, knowing I'll be looking at camera feed to verify. And if you didn't do it, I apologize, but whoever did better come forward."

Steve shook his head, then he turned and started walking off. Obviously, whatever problem Steve had was Steve's problem. And while Fernando felt bad for the guy, it wasn't his responsibility. Everyone else remained standing where they were, and where Fernando had once feared judgment, he now only felt acceptance.

Ricky waved his hand. "Now skedaddle! There's food to be eaten, and we're going to have some music a little later. Let's give these lovebirds a little privacy."

Then Ricky grabbed Shane's arm, steering him toward the food table. "And you let them be. There's nothing wrong with a little smooching. Especially when there's some apologizing to do and a life to plan."

Fernando looked down at Nicole. "I guess I have

more than just a little apologizing to do. Can you forgive me for being such a fool?"

She pulled him closer to her. "As long as you don't make me wait too long to marry you. We've wasted enough time with all this nonsense."

"Absolutely," Fernando said, kissing her again. "It's time to move forward with our lives, wherever that takes us."

With Nicole in his arms, Fernando had no doubt that whatever happened, he could handle it with such a strong woman by his side.

Epilogue

Nicole looked out the window to see Fernando pulling in with a horse trailer behind him.

"What are you doing?" she asked when she ran out of the house to greet him. "You were supposed to be picking up your suit for the wedding tomorrow, not messing around. I thought Ricky was giving you the day off."

He grinned at her. "He did. I had some errands to run besides getting my suit. Come see."

Fernando led her around the back of the horse trailer. "I've been talking to Walt, my old mentor from prison, and he's been keeping an eye out for me for any good mustangs coming in. And I think we finally found the perfect companion for Snookie. Meet Elmer."

The bay gelding looked almost like he could have been Snookie's brother. Fernando opened the trailer and led him out. As Nicole petted him, she could sense there was something special about him. And, as Snookie came to the fence and whinnied, Nicole could tell that Snookie agreed.

Since the incident that had landed Nicole in the hospital, Snookie hadn't bitten anyone. In fact, most people wouldn't have known that Snookie had been such a problem horse. They'd even let the boys ride on her a time or two.

But, with Shane and Leah's wedding coming up, and Leah and the boys moving in with Shane, Shane's horses would be going back to Shane's house. Which meant Snookie needed a friend. Nicole hadn't known what they were going to do, but Fernando had told her to have a little faith that things would work out.

"Have you been planning this all along?"

He grinned. "I've been talking a lot with Walt about my experience postrelease, and he's been helping me understand why my adjustment has been so rough. I'm also helping him better prepare the men he's got in the program now to understand how to handle the kind of rejection I face. Most important, he's been helping me search for the perfect friend for Snookie. I'd hoped to find one sooner, but it's taken a lot longer than I thought. Still, I think he's worth the wait. I've never met a horse with a sweeter disposition."

As opposed to Snookie's moodiness, which was why training her had been such a challenge.

Nicole gave Elmer another pat, then led him over to the corral where Snookie was.

The two horses sniffed at each other cautiously, but then Snookie gave Elmer the playful nudge she liked to give to indicate her acceptance. When Elmer nudged Snookie back, Nicole thought she saw little hearts in his eyes.

Okay, so maybe that was total fancy on her part, but she had a good feeling about these two and their relationship. Even though she'd hoped for a companion for Snookie sooner, she'd learned her lesson with Snookie and had been willing to wait until Fernando found the right horse.

Which was exactly how it had ended up for her own relationship. She looked over at the man she loved and would be marrying tomorrow. Waiting for Fernando to work things out on his own had given him a confidence in himself that she couldn't have given him. She knew beyond a shadow of a doubt that he loved her and would always fight for her.

Even though Fernando had feared how people would react to his record, not only had he gained a number of private training clients, but other outfits had tried stealing Fernando from Ricky. However, Ricky and Fernando had a deep bond, and as Nicole glanced down at the turquoise ring on her finger, she knew that they'd become the family each other needed.

Ricky pulled into the driveway, as if he'd known she was thinking about him.

"What do you think of the horse? Did Walt have anything for me?" he asked, leaning out the window.

Before Nicole could answer, Ricky jumped out of his truck and came over to where they were standing, watching the horses.

"You sure you don't want me to give you away tomorrow?" Ricky asked.

Nicole shook her head. "I'm sure. My sisters and nephews are going to walk me down the aisle, and there won't be anyone giving anyone away, but a joining of hearts that make a family bigger and stronger."

Then she looked over at him and smiled. "But if you

want to be part of our family and walk with us, we'd be honored to have you."

Pastor Roberts had thought the idea strange at first, but the more they talked about it, he came to realize it would be a moving symbol of the value of families growing through marriage, rather than viewing it as a separation.

It would be weird, with Leah moving in with Shane, Nicole moving in with Fernando and Erin being by herself in the ranch house. But with everyone still so close, none of them would be far from each other at all.

Ricky gave her a funny look, then nodded. "I like the sound of that. Maybe you should all change your last name to Ruiz, then when you have a baby, its name can start with an R and carry on the Double R legacy."

Nicole tried not to groan. Ricky kept reminding them that he wasn't getting any younger, and that since he'd messed up his own chance at grandbabies, he wanted to enjoy their babies, so they'd better hurry up and start having some.

But as they'd all learned over the past few months, the best things came with patience, time and love, and whatever the future brought, Nicole trusted that it would be wonderful. Not because they wouldn't face anything bad, but because they had each other.

* * * * *

*Pick up Leah and Shane's story,
the first book in Danica Favorite's
Three Sisters Ranch miniseries:*

Her Cowboy Inheritance

Available now from Love Inspired!

*Find more great reads at
www.LoveInspired.com*

Dear Reader,

While all of the characters and situations in this book are purely the work of my imagination, I wanted this book to honor the amazing folks in the federal corrections system who train wild mustangs, who are then sold and used by the general public. Our family has gotten to know a number of fantastic horses who came from this program, so when it was time to get our own mustangs, we knew that's where we'd get them. These programs help both horse and human on so many levels, and I love being able to share just a little about them.

Though I've never been to prison, I've seen how it's affected people I care about, and I also know that many of us, like Fernando, feel trapped by our pasts. God never meant for any of us to live in shame, and as Fernando and Nicole learned, we need to learn to trust God to bring us healing, especially as it often comes from unexpected places.

Wherever you're at in life, I pray God will bring you healing for whatever you need, and you will find the freedom that comes from love.

I love connecting with my readers, so be sure to find me online:

Newsletter: *http://eepurl.com/7HCXj*
Website: *http://www.danicafavorite.com/*
Twitter: *https://Twitter.com/danicafavorite*
Instagram: *https://www.Instagram.com/danicafavorite/*
Facebook: *https://www.Facebook.com/danicafavorite-author*

Amazon: *https://www.Amazon.com/danica-favorite/e/ B00KRP0IFU*
BookBub: *https://www.BookBub.com/authors/danica-favorite*

Sending love to you and yours,
Danica Favorite

Get 4 FREE REWARDS!

We'll send you 2 FREE Books plus 2 FREE Mystery Gifts.

Love Inspired® books feature contemporary inspirational romances with Christian characters facing the challenges of life and love.

FREE Value Over **$20**

YES! Please send me 2 FREE Love Inspired® Romance novels and my 2 FREE mystery gifts (gifts are worth about $10 retail). After receiving them, if I don't wish to receive any more books, I can return the shipping statement marked "cancel." If I don't cancel, I will receive 6 brand-new novels every month and be billed just $5.24 for the regular-print edition or $5.74 each for the larger-print edition in the U.S., or $5.74 each for the regular-print edition or $6.24 each for the larger-print edition in Canada. That's a savings of at least 13% off the cover price. It's quite a bargain! Shipping and handling is just 50¢ per book in the U.S. and 75¢ per book in Canada.* I understand that accepting the 2 free books and gifts places me under no obligation to buy anything. I can always return a shipment and cancel at any time. The free books and gifts are mine to keep no matter what I decide.

Choose one: ☐ **Love Inspired® Romance Regular-Print** (105/305 IDN GMY4)   ☐ **Love Inspired® Romance Larger-Print** (122/322 IDN GMY4)

Name (please print)

Address   Apt. #

City   State/Province   Zip/Postal Code

Mail to the Reader Service:
IN U.S.A.: P.O. Box 1341, Buffalo, NY 14240-8531
IN CANADA: P.O. Box 603, Fort Erie, Ontario L2A 5X3

Want to try 2 free books from another series? Call 1-800-873-8635 or visit www.ReaderService.com.

SPECIAL EXCERPT FROM

What happens when the nanny harbors a secret that could change everything?

Read on for a sneak preview of
The Nanny's Secret Baby,
the next book in Lee Tobin McClain's
Redemption Ranch miniseries.

Any day she could see Sammy was a good day. But she was pretty sure Jack was about to turn down her nanny offer. And then she'd have to tell Penny she couldn't take the apartment, and leave.

The thought of being away from her son after spending precious time with him made her chest ache, and she blinked away unexpected tears as she approached Jack and Sammy.

Sammy didn't look up at her. He was holding up one finger near his own face, moving it back and forth.

Jack caught his hand. "Say hi, Sammy! Here's Aunt Arianna."

Sammy tugged his hand away and continued to move his finger in front of his face.

"Sammy, come on."

Sammy turned slightly away from his father and refocused on his fingers.

"It's okay," Arianna said, because she could see the beginnings of a meltdown. "He doesn't need to greet me. What's up?"

"Look," he said, "I've been thinking about what you said." He rubbed a hand over the back of his neck, clearly uncomfortable.

Sammy's hand moved faster, and he started humming a wordless tune. It was almost as if he could sense the tension between Arianna and Jack.

"It's okay, Jack," she said. "I get it. My being your nanny was a foolish idea." Foolish, but oh so appealing. She ached to pick

Sammy up and hold him, to know that she could spend more time with him, help him learn, get him support for his special needs.

But it wasn't her right.

"Actually," he said, "that's what I wanted to talk about. It does seem sort of foolish, but…I think I'd like to offer you the job."

She stared at him, her eyes filling. "Oh, Jack," she said, her voice coming out in a whisper. Had he really just said she could have the job?

Behind her, the rumble and snap of tables being folded and chairs being stacked, the cheerful conversation of parishioners and community people, faded to an indistinguishable murmur.

She was going to be able to be with her son. Every day. She reached out and stroked Sammy's soft hair, and even though he ignored her touch, her heart nearly melted with the joy of being close to him.

Jack's brow wrinkled. "On a trial basis," he said. "Just for the rest of the summer, say."

Of course. She pulled her hand away from Sammy and drew in a deep breath. She needed to calm down and take things one step at a time. Yes, leaving him at the end of the summer would break her heart ten times more. But even a few weeks with her son was more time than she deserved.

With God all things are possible. The pastor had said it, and she'd just witnessed its truth. She was being given a job, the care of her son and a place to live.

It was a blessing, a huge one. But it came at a cost: she was going to need to conceal the truth from Jack on a daily basis. And given the way her heart was jumping around in her chest, she wondered if she was going to be able to survive this much of God's blessing.

Don't miss
The Nanny's Secret Baby *by Lee Tobin McClain,*
available August 2019 wherever
Love Inspired® books and ebooks are sold.

www.LoveInspired.com

LIEXP0719

Looking for inspiration in tales
of hope, faith and heartfelt romance?

Check out **Love Inspired**® and
Love Inspired® **Suspense** books!

New books available every month!

CONNECT WITH US AT:

Facebook.com/groups/HarlequinConnection

Facebook.com/HarlequinBooks

Twitter.com/HarlequinBooks

Instagram.com/HarlequinBooks

Pinterest.com/HarlequinBooks

ReaderService.com